WERT AND THE LIFE WITHOUT END

OTHER WORKS BY CLAUDE OLLIER IN ENGLISH TRANSLATION

The Mise-en-Scène

Law and Order

Disconnection

WERT AND THE LIFE WITHOUT END
CLAUDE OLLIER

TRANSLATED BY URSULA MEANY SCOTT

DALKEY ARCHIVE PRESS
CHAMPAIGN • DUBLIN • LONDON

Originally published in French as *Wert et la vie sans fin* by P.O.L éditeur, 2007

First edition, 2011

Library of Congress Cataloging-in-Publication Data

Ollier, Claude.
[Wert et la vie sans fin. English]
Wert and the life without end / Claude Ollier ; translated by Ursula Meany Scott.
p. cm.
"Originally published in French as Wert et la vie sans fin by P.O.L editeur, 2007."
ISBN 978-1-56478-626-5 (pbk. : alk. paper)
I. Scott, Ursula Meany. II. Title.
PQ2675.L398W4713 2011
843'.914--dc22

2011012775

Partially funded by the University of Illinois at Urbana-Champaign and by a grant from the Illinois Arts Council, a state agency

Ouvrage publié avec le concours du Ministère français chargé de la culture - Centre national du livre

This work has been published, in part, thanks to the French Ministry of Culture - National Book Center

www.dalkeyarchive.com

Cover: design and composition by Danielle Dutton, illustration by Nicholas Motte
Printed on permanent/durable acid-free paper and bound in the United States of America

I

Withdrawal

—the image

Full moon—and this long rectangle of light on the carpet, blocking my passage.

I remained on the edge of this incursion of whiteness that was spread out like chalk dust over the carpet.

The word incursion is in keeping with the unpredictability of the moment; I wasn't expecting such an obstacle, that's all.

Rectangle of moon blocking my passage, a void at my feet.

My legs wouldn't take the plunge, that's all there is to it.

Then I went through the door and into the office.

I don't come here often, but this is where my memories are.

I feel comfortable here, though it's unclear what I'm meant to be doing; there's a file on the table to the left, a mauve file, that's all, I open the file.

Close it.

There's nothing in the file.

Once in a while somebody important shows up here too, in front of the table, a soldier perhaps, in civilian clothes, or a civilian, thin, stooping, hands me an article from a specialist journal to read, or a report announcing some major upcoming event for the unit.

Remains standing, watching for my reaction.

It was obviously a question of an exceptional military event, I thought it best to say nothing, acknowledging the moment's importance with my silence.

Builders of empires, cities, and temples: distant voyages, great adventures.

My boss seemed to gauge my reaction, I remained motionless and kept my mouth shut.

The atmosphere of the room seems familiar, this file on the left, empty, someone's done this to me before, I can't think where, the memory a rustle, a breath.

The file on the left, and me right-handed! something from the past?

To study the emptiness in the file, to flesh it out, were you lord of this realm?

What did you do, what did you invent in your realm? The other is here, the one who's waiting, I ignore what he expects of me, he's no longer waiting, he's no longer here now.

It's an office I don't go to regularly, this ill-defined job, sometimes one page, two pages in the file, reminding me that for a long time now there's been something or other I was supposed to check, to settle, piece together, report, none of it urgent, going on for such a long time now, how long exactly?

Not many employees, incidentally; often I don't meet a single one; the boss will suddenly appear, that's all.

I sit down in the rickety armchair, its arms, its feet decorated with hunting scenes, with lions, I take the file on the left and open it.

Once, I found a large drawing inside, arabesques and coarse lines, intertwined and daunting, imprinted, what I had to do was read it, read the curves, the angles, make sense of it, or just to contemplate it, to etch it on my mind.

Release—all my time.

Or else I have to turn up here every day because it really is my job, my post, periods of time in this office like expeditions, campaigns. A few pages on the table in the beginning I think; I spread them out, pretended to be doing something, revised them, turned them every which way.

Did what was important.

They related to former actions, feats of arms and of thought, capabilities, the gloss wearing thin in the process, every piece of the jigsaw on the table in the end.

Everything laid out flat at a given moment, staggered arrangements and spatial hierarchies.

It was no doubt like this at the beginning, turn and turn again, and put back, replace the pages, the image would appear then disappear, reappear, the image of the one who always used to come back, go again, come back, and sweep me along, I was sure he would always come back.

And he'd relate what had happened in the interval, seasons having passed, he'd changed his name, reappeared, we'd leave again on some escapade together, ordeals often imposed, we'd delight in this imposition, this chance for life, coming face-to-face with death's burning eyes.

Changed his name, was this really the same red-blooded guy, with the same drive, same zeal for risk, danger, taking up the gauntlet?

Must be a file on that, somewhere.

In my spare time I pace up and down the dimly lit corridors, somewhat furtively, some days the light increases a little, the night just seems to vanish, the light errant, elusive.

Corridors painted dark brown, almost bronze in the grooves between the woodwork, some gray here and there, the floorboards creak, an occasional strip of carpet, a stretch of muffled tread, a door opens, you didn't hear it open, someone pokes their head out.

Follows with their eyes.

The corridors go the whole way around the building, there's a right angle, then a dark area always dissuades me from going any farther, what good is it to go farther if it's to go round in a circle?

He has never come here, has never had to come, such was his luck, headed off on adventures, set forth or engaged in battles, waging war.

Roaming the forests, the parched plains, the steppes full of wild animals.

Sweeping me along.

Wüst, some would say, others *Wolf*, by mistake, through confusion, but *Wild* was his name.

Wild—it's still his name, will forever be his name—never dealt with the office and its ill-defined, irregular work, never had to deal with it, I hadn't dealt with it either as long as Wild was here, I came when he disappeared.

Lured, summoned perhaps, or else of my own free will, as though inevitably, called by what, no idea how, pushed in a most natural manner, guided by whom, all in all I was no longer myself.

It must have been part of my illness, absences of self, disoriented or overwhelmed, unreasonable, roaming outdoors then finding myself here, at least it's quieter here.

Sheltered from view, from words, from noise, far from city and headquarters, quieter here and the files keep you busy, this vague work, solitary, with no fixed term, that's what they told me, what else were they going to say?

A treacherous, unremitting hold, vicelike, tightening, body in a creeping paralysis.

Hoarse breath, then silent breath.

Motionless and silent, my eye on these papers, the hours spent turning them every which way.

What was this business, administration, organization, ministry; this work was new to me.

Caught off guard, lost right from the outset, left alone in this place more often than not, began not showing up, one day, two days, days on end, considered not coming back for a long time, what rhyme or reason to this job, a subjection, this devotion to fulfilling it, sometimes considered never returning.

The vice tightened suddenly, seizing me every moment, every night, every thought of dreaming.

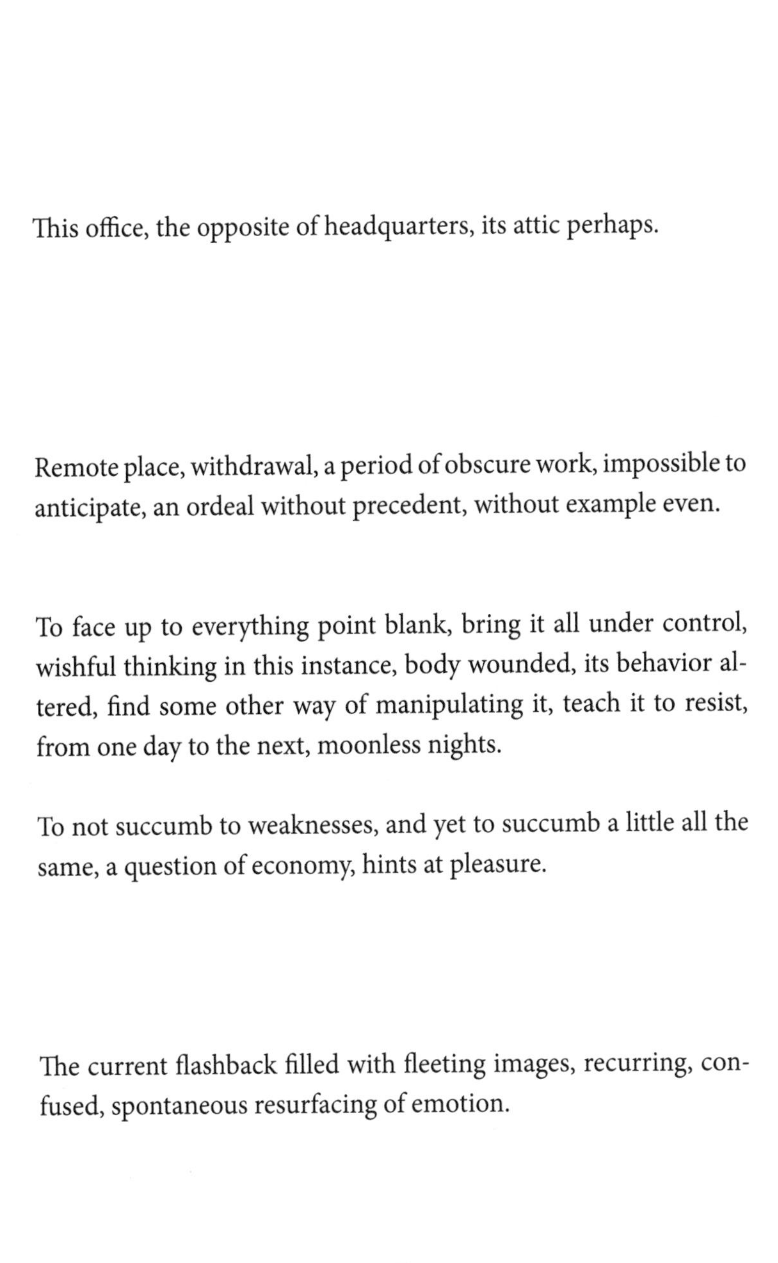

This office, the opposite of headquarters, its attic perhaps.

Remote place, withdrawal, a period of obscure work, impossible to anticipate, an ordeal without precedent, without example even.

To face up to everything point blank, bring it all under control, wishful thinking in this instance, body wounded, its behavior altered, find some other way of manipulating it, teach it to resist, from one day to the next, moonless nights.

To not succumb to weaknesses, and yet to succumb a little all the same, a question of economy, hints at pleasure.

The current flashback filled with fleeting images, recurring, confused, spontaneous resurfacing of emotion.

Scenes of glory come to mind, great moments, skirmishes, victories, must keep them far from oneself, elude the snare, never waver.

Should imagine them as fixed images, etchings from times past, colors faded, brightness dulled.

Images glimpsed from a distant life, a thoughtful look, curious but no more than that, affected some days, unsettled as necessary, perhaps even a little entertained.

Scares, starts, terror, so who were those two then, neither him nor me!

Crumpled features, barely readable, and yet they look like us.

Reckless conquerors, we were sent over there, restless, suspect, brothers in arms.

Snapshots of times we were on reconnaissance, the city and its surrounding forests, no cedars or fig trees, just pines as far as the eye could see, sand paths, the two of us side by side on a sand track between the rows of pines in the endless forest circling the city, the risk posed by every bend, ditch, and fork.

Wild, his hatchet and rifle carving the way, slicing a space in which to move and breathe and laugh, stealthily through the thickets, all his senses on the alert, knew how to gain ground quickly as well, sometimes I was incapable of following him.

He'd ease his pace, wouldn't take off ahead, though bigger and stronger than I was, let me catch up, he was my shield, my guard.

Would still support me, comfort me, coax me along, if only he was here, god damn it! Would talk to me, deliver me again.

Insanity brought on by this place, so isolated, all the things that go through your head, disarray of the heart and of ideas, nonsense, desires out of place and out of season.

The only one who can deliver you is yourself, get that into your head, besides you know it full well, stop whining, grieving, moaning.

Think about others for a change!

Sometimes he appears there in the morning, the stooped, thin one, in front of the table or even sitting, head in hands, leaning over on the empty file, appears to be asleep, gets up when he hears me, offers me a daily paper, a pamphlet, read that why don't you, he says.

Or a weekly paper, never any books, I pretend to read, rumors from headquarters, saber-rattling, wars on the other side of the world, floods, assaults, rapes.

Current affairs, color photos, muffled sequence of sounds from the city, restless suburbs, famines, distant rumblings from poor districts.

Rainy weather forecast, every image dull and white, everything exceptional leaking away, what am I supposed to do with these newspapers, how are they supposed to help me?

A weary renewal each morning, dreaded, I face it enthusiastically, believe it or not, nothing you can do to fight off something so intrusively and overwhelmingly irreversible, heart and arteries, the wave of black blood.

I go through the door and into the office, up the stairs, no bell, nothing on the door, no nameplate, no name, push open the door, it closes by itself.

The office is separated from the rest of the premises by a partition halfway up the walls, a room that's not at all too narrow, plain, with nothing on the walls, no orders or regulations, notices.

Ink stains on the table that have evidently been scraped off, unpolished, metal lamp to the right, I pull the small chain and the dimmed light makes a circle on the scratched wood, the file's on the left, or the folder rather, notes are slipped inside it, pages from notepads, ought to get to work on them, nobody says anything to me, no reason for any hurry.

A steward with lowered eyes spoke to me of compensation if I'd make a deal, of bonuses, allowances, that was in the beginning; I didn't ask for anything, of course, money has no bearing on this story, economics settled by means of other bargaining chips, a higher price, you get into debt quickly here.

Didn't come back again, made a mistake no doubt, confused me with someone, got the wrong office, the wrong client, wrong method.

Wrong story.

I was too afraid to knock on doors, introduce myself, appear, salute, deep down I've no interest in that, pouring my heart out, have no desire to talk, talk about misfortune, torment, sorrows, listen to other people's woes, listen to other people, their lives.

Listen at doors.

No common language, weights or measures, things sorted out somewhere between body and voice, the sounds of the body, its complaints, so different between bodies that the things have no common words.

Sorted out body to body.

All outbursts, fits of temper, and screams banished, permanent silence reigns, a great respect for others, here the meeting place of the silent ones, the taciturn, the discreet.

The building of the withdrawn ones, the most secret, those who keep to themselves, solve their problems alone, solve things within themselves, keep it all inside, the heartbreak, collapse, turmoil of feeling and delirium.

The building of the battered, the numbed, those who've never recovered, minds lost, they go on sitting in a corner, no longer say anything, no longer go anywhere.

Stricken for life, shut away inside themselves, emptied, surrounded by paleness, pale shadows, such is the fate of the living who must still live.

Tough for adventurers, for troopers, hunters, for those who like to roam, to wander, to lose themselves and never retrace their steps, tough spending all that time with scenes recurring before your eyes every day, every night within your dreams.

All energy captive, trained to remember.

Recurrence of images whose lines are blurred, shots frozen in time, places marked unobtrusively, established, fixed, scenes without characters sometimes, only perspective and landscape with the ambient flavor of earth and season, still and slow skies.

Dense clouds floating high above that region of our first exploits, clouds stretched so their fine tendrils and frills clipped the blue expanse of sky, great winter cold weighing on the cluster of tall trees, the sandstone, the dense pine needles.

The weapons fell silent for entire days with the frost, lips chapped under stiff fingers, we didn't leave the bivouac, irregulars buried beneath snow and winds, cut off from the world.

The target was that fort in the center of the forest, unprecedented challenge to use sapper tunnels to get close to and destroy it, the low country, the rivers, the fate of the town and peace of the country all depended on our succeeding.

I was passionately interested in books about science and adventure, known for my exploits, well-read but actively involved, often inclined to meditation, daydreaming, idleness even.

Subject to absences.

At other moments greedy for pleasures, unruly, wild, the pleasure-seeker of my clan, a real desperado.

These contrasting moods weren't at all conflicting, they lived off one another, stimulated one another, swapped hands, I used to sense instantly when their tide turned.

Lust, study, they went hand in hand, and debauchery, fighting.

Some of those in the city were envious or jealous of me, said I was tyrannical, offended them, I'd take the darkness of my knowledge far away, would yield the ground to them, subject my body to exhaustion, to trickery, to danger.

I joined up at the front line, filled with an enthusiasm that came from storybook gallantry, pleased to have an opportunity to live the hard life, of a diversion from the exacting pace of my work.

Irregular force up on the heights at the edge of the enormous forest, my men at my command, I awaited the moment, and they my signal, ready for the charge.

That night the enemy squadrons were flying over the town in dense, repeated waves, machines invisible in the darkness between the stars, armor-clad, with decoys, projectiles going astray, burning the stubble fields, others setting the roofs alight, laying waste to temples and museums, palaces, libraries.

The storm past, ignoring the glow on the plain in the distance, I had fallen asleep.

A dream at dawn chilled me to the bone.

The story stops there, at the top of a blank page.

I found the pages in the file again this morning, was no longer thinking about them, they hadn't been there for a long time, that's for sure, where were they?

It's certainly my handwriting.

The Boss had encouraged me, in uniform that day, no holding back he'd said, no obligations, this'll help you, it's the only thing that'll help you in your state.

Kept them in his possession all this time, has he even read them, the first lines, skimmed through at best, may have made a copy of them, in what way have they made my job easier, mine or his?

I reread them, it's definitely my style, but certain words surprise me, caprices, infatuations, dissoluteness.

Was I really talking about myself, without a doubt yes.

No corrections in the margins, no comments at the top of the page, no praise or criticism, he hasn't graded me, though that's what would really help, if something ought to help me, a good grade, for diligence.

Put them back there so I can continue, finish them at least, would've filed them otherwise, or torn them up, thrown them in the wastepaper basket.

Never had me come to his office, summoned or invited, where is his office, at what point in the corridor, which open corner, a panoramic view over the whole floor?

There was that dream, it's true, I'd forgotten that dream, he was right to encourage me.

There were two dreams, weren't there?

What am I doing in the corridor instead of searching, reassembling, rereading these dreams, unraveling them, rewriting them?

He would have cut out the bit about the dream, kept it for himself, censored it in his own way, what does he blame me for?

Lack of attention, of concentration, a tendency toward carelessness? it's a good lesson.

I turned at a right angle at the end of the corridor, carried on without thinking, preoccupied by this business, took a few more steps in that corridor, nose to the ground.

Better lit than before, it's no longer shadowy, there are names on some doors, names that mean nothing to me, no rank, no job title.

Out of secrecy or disorganization, or pretense, is that man really behind the door, or does he only come in from time to time perhaps, usually stays away.

Or there may never have been anyone behind the door.

Empty office, empty mind, obsessed and suddenly empty, or ready to explode, rebellious, assaulted.

Resistant to this test, struggling to act, too much suffering, a cruel fate.

Take up the work where I left off, right at the start perhaps, revolt is part of the work, and rebellion, and cruel fate, torment.

If only Wild could see.

To pinpoint the place in the forest, the exact place, to describe this place I've so often recalled makes the pain even harder to bear.

Nights of bombardments, mind alert, all thoughts intensified.

I found myself again at the end of the corridor, which is better lit than usual, had never gone to the end of the corridor, it used to be too dark.

Had never noticed that office with the swinging door that seems deserted, unoccupied at least, nothing on the door and nothing behind.

I listened, on my guard, pushed the door, the increased light from the corridor lit the room a little, revealed a filing cabinet, an armchair, where was the chair then, the desk?

Quiet place, as though isolated from others, the infrequency of activity upstairs would make every part of it quiet, what's more this one didn't look onto the stairwell, wasn't a thoroughfare.

I closed the door again and retraced my steps, turned at the angle of the corridor, got back to my office.

The sheets still in the folder, the last one almost blank, was up to me to fill it, fill others, how many others?

Starting this page was posing a problem, I couldn't find the words, Wild would've found the words to start, though he was the uneducated one, the barbarian, didn't really know words, the few he did know, knew how to say.

With him gone, I disappointed the words, they defied me, made me a victim, were no longer familiar to me—me, the scholarly one—they no longer respected me.

Would've found the words needed to recount the things that happened next and the dreams, in my desolation every term that comes to mind only results in apathy, in distrust.

I felt myself falling asleep, falling asleep here? my head wobbled slightly, barely moved, a thought brushed across my mind that I might never have seen either pencil or eraser on the desk, it brushed across the desk and room ignoring that I was sitting there sinking, no more grief, no more torture, I was no longer there anymore.

The Boss is at my side now, in a blue ceremonial uniform, do I call you Sir? I'm the Quartermaster, call me Quartermaster now.

I went to the end of the corridor, saw the door was open, pushed it, saw the other room there in the other corridor beyond the corner, I'd like to move there.

To work there, Quartermaster.

I'd be able to concentrate better, I'd really be by myself, I'd only think about that, my work there, better off being isolated, better to really be alone.

Would only think about that, the beginning, those dreams.

They're filed in that room there, the dreams, buried, listed as in a palace bedroom, gilded paneling, a four-poster bed perhaps, a heavy carved door.

It will be necessary to put in a lock.

Just then I saw something again, the figure came out into the light, not enough for me to identify it.

A large-bodied figure, stocky, built like a rock.

To clarify, Quartermaster, I'd move there permanently.

He looks at the bare wall facing him as though he'd just seen something important written on it, eyes fixed, upright body imperceptibly relaxed in its posture, his lips move a little, barely curving, a long way from smiling.

I've been expecting this from you for some time, he said simply.

Already walking ahead of me through the corridor, mauve file in hand, pencil and eraser, once we've reached the right place he pushes open the door.

Presses the button on the doorframe and a white light takes possession of the room, I notice the desk hunched back into a corner and a seat as well, an armchair cloaked in a worn gray cover.

He pulls the table to the center of the room, places the objects on it, says that the lighting system's an automatic time switch, five minutes of light, enough to note down what's in one's head each time.

On leaving, hands me the key, a nondescript key, here I'll be undisturbed, not too many people in the institution at the moment.

Once he left, I sat in the armchair and the bulb went out almost immediately, I could see the light from the corridor under the door, the sliver penetrated as far as the chair, as far as the table legs.

I remained seated, stretched out a bit, what else was there to do, it was the position most suited to contemplation, motionless, at ease, deprived of light.

Everything was played out between the eye and the simple geometrical coordinates offered by the room's minimal decoration; I'd chosen it, I wasn't about to complain, still the other office was more modern.

A desk on which to do everything, narrow, high legs, a kitchen chair, the filing cabinet with sliding drawers, its slides dusty, an old model, what's in there, can it even be opened?

No window, naturally, a closed, blind space was necessary, neither transom nor skylight.

It was neither warmer nor cooler than in the corridors or at the other end of the floor near the stairs, which let in a little air despite everything.

With no possibility of sleep, exhausted for no reason, I avoided sinking into a kind of mindless state, indifference or lethargy, you're not here to daydream, I told myself again.

To form a stimulating image in my mind was necessary, in my state, said the Quartermaster Boss, didn't say in my depression, I appreciated the nuance, how tactfully I'm treated here, such courtesy compensates for the absence of comfort.

After all, I might have spent months traipsing around the streets, wandering through the night, getting upset, getting drunk alone.

Losing my way, ending up in bad neighborhoods, being attacked, being injured.

Too disoriented to behave correctly outside, to wander around as if nothing was up, to meet people, speak, use a detached tone, not let anything show.

Here was refuge.

The unpardonable strikes like lightning, shatters with a couple of words the composure of which you boast, this imperturbability on which you compliment yourself with such great casualness of reflection and manner.

The indigestible.

Lord above, what did you do? reason falters at the harshness of your edicts, the cruelty of your heart!

Emphatic words confusing the direction of my quest, and how was I to dispel them, the banalities of circumstance inform feeling much more than they express it.

The bareness of the place didn't preclude the development of connections, quite the opposite, the rarefaction of objects suits this development, these connections are strengthened by deprivations, by exclusions, by absences.

They would open up in the vacuity of the space.

They became perceptible after a moment, running between the unassuming, solid, yet loose arrangement of the furnishings, they sprang up from the corners of the room, slipped along the walls, I observed the development of these minute tropisms and invisible translations, pretended to bear witness but nothing more, knew that my body was the catalyst that set them in motion, neither invented nor created them but triggered their dance, they've been there since space and time swapped the hands they were dealt in this place.

Are there permanently, always waiting for the next occupant, a new man to rule the room or one returning, affected, breathing a new life into these corners.

The returning one carries the connections within him, imprinted from his first stay, they leave their mark on his muscles, his nerves, invest his body with unexpected recollections, sudden attractions between places from the past frequented spontaneously, voluntarily or otherwise, through desire or constraint.

Terrors, dread of well-known paths being cleared, resurgences of things long stored, buried signals sleeping in matter, quietly hibernating.

A wave as though born on the weak tide of light outlined the shadow of a garden with a path lined with yew trees and a great many stones piled up and scattered across the path.

I'm coming from the spot where there's a well, moving around the well I see the stones, they take up the whole space between the gate and the apple tree, I lift them one by one and throw them to the right, to the left, hard as I can.

And my men are there, they're watching the scene, motionless in a circle, encouraging me, congratulating me.

And that's the dream at dawn, the dream after those lights all night long and the smoke coming off the plain, the smell of burned rocks, of bodies.

There was another dream, the night after perhaps, the two dreams preceded his coming, his bursting into the camp, and the confrontation, you'd think he'd been fired at me.

Trained, incited against me.

I found it difficult to get up from the armchair where I'd ended up completely stretched out after gradually slipping down, to drag myself as far as the door, drawn by the beam of light, I groped around for a moment then pressed the button and the burst of light made me recoil as though assaulted by a terrible noise, but there was no noise in the corridor and in the room even less.

I should've prepared myself, had only five minutes to take down the dream of stones on the path.

The five minutes seemed long to me, what sense do I have of duration from here on in, and what's a minute worth here in this time of reflection and murmuring voices, the bulb in the ceiling doesn't give out much light, I have some difficulty finding the page where I stopped again.

The same place on the page.

The too-sharp pencil punctures the paper, it's not the same pencil, it's been sharpened excessively.

I began, the words turned away, I hunted them down and set them on the paper, wrote them then crossed them out, it didn't start well, my dream.

I took great care, the anxiety set in once more, would the light go out, I would go unhurriedly as far as the door and press the button, what was the problem?

Really, this dream is short, garden, well, and apple tree, the path, the stones as far as the railings, all that was left was the crowd, my men surrounding me congratulating, encouraging, was reaching the end of it when the darkness came again.

Getting up, missed the door, then found the doorframe and pressed the button and nothing happened, no more light, pressed ten times at various intervals, the dense substance, this darkness, filled the room exactly, didn't bury it, kept it silently in its possession, unchanging, homogeneous, still, with neither internal flux nor tension in any point of its volume.

Nothing was hurrying me any longer, why was I rushing earlier, I found the armchair again feeling my way along, sleepwalking with arms outstretched disregarding the straight line.

Back wedged against the leather backrest, swiveling rectangle of scuffed, dirty leather, arms lying on the armrests, unsteady strips of leather under the elbows, relaxed legs stretched out straight in a classic attitude of repose, staring at the ceiling, I waited for what would come next.

The continuation of events in the narrow room, chosen office or second office, and simultaneously the continuation of past episodes that chose themselves in light of the recent dream—forming, from then on, a continuation.

A colored reactant is applied to the story of life, selects scenes from this drama in a trail of fire, assigns them an exclusive, emotional, extraordinary coefficient.

Wild had appeared not long after the dreams, as though they had inserted him into the edge of the wood that overlooked the town, my camp in the vanguard up there surrounded by dangers, wild animals, bears, wolves, isolated partisans stubbornly resisting any contact or discipline.

A rumor was spreading that a lone-wolf was waging his own futile battle, come from steppe to pasture, carrying out some kind of personal war, moving around this region on intimate terms with earth and beast, plants and waters.

Rumor like clouds massing, gathering strength, the boredom of the camp lends itself to that.

Legend taking shape as happens during exceptional times like these, what this had to do with the fortress in the center of the forest remained undetermined.

Gossip, a word repeated, altered, the adventure seized with both hands, the story continues.

A slip of the tongue is enough to clinch the deal.

I'm here talking to myself in the room that's now lit up, did I close my eyes while thinking those words, you don't sleep here, don't dream, drowse at best, when did the light come back?

Partial light, I'll end up finding it beautiful.

The Quartermaster knocked perhaps, came in, without answer pressed the button, saw me considering the words to describe this encounter, gently closed the door.

I'd closed the door!

It's still closed, the key in the lock, mechanism not working properly, outdated or not looked after, very uncooperative.

Damned time switch.

Is it blocked, allowing my eye to run incessantly from one surface to the other of this little room where neither form nor color delight.

Functional place, bound to an austerity, minimal harshness, no ugliness, everything is conducive to work, to the tension of the mind.

Nothing should be discouraging, all the same.

A discipline I'd consented to, didn't you come of your own free will? here the ideal place, nothing distracts, all diversions or misbehavior out of the question, futility of making a scene, that the work should come to an end, quickly and efficiently carried out, some never succeed, pass away tormented, revolted, appalled to death.

Footsteps in the corridor, not the Quartermaster's measured, confident ones, these are shorter and uneven, hesitating in front of the door, who's putting a name on this door now and what would my name mean to anyone who'll read it?

The steps move away, I hear them for a long time, came from the reception office, the room I left over there or the first office, I used to hear the steps often in the stairway over there, someone sometimes turned the doorknob, a head poked in fleetingly, disappeared.

Who's wandering around at this hour, what walker in the corridor here, regular resident coming back from a stroll or precursor of a new batch of guests, lured by the premises, or just souls in torment?

The stumbling walk returns, fades, I hurry to the door, turn the key, the corridor is empty, I was too slow getting up.

Weak light in the corridor, or so it seemed, my one light staying on would seem brighter, I venture as far as the corner that I haven't turned yet, second corner after the first office, what was the prowler going to do around here, scout out the area, reserve a room, must have wandered over from that side.

Got scared, didn't find reception again, so many right angles however, how could you get lost, you'd have to really want to here.

I passed the corner and followed a new corridor with paneling and worn, fitted carpet, weak bulb in the ceiling every ten steps only, closed doors, nowhere a name, silence behind the doors, where they heard me, held their breath.

The passage narrows, furniture piled up on the right, on the left, dumped or stacked up erratically against the walls, necessitating detours, twisting one's body, furniture in the course of being stowed, relocated, what is this mess?

Tables, wastepaper baskets, filing cabinets, and chairs, lights wrapped in white paper, laid out like mummies in parallel rows, barely space to slide between them.

Rarefied air, I breathe again, did I or didn't I finish writing down that dream, garden and stones, my men in a circle on the path, I ought to have checked.

Must wait a while, the other dream was nearby, a tangible place, diaphanous, and its weight of emotion, phantom scene tamed close by, you get hotter then colder searching for it, it'll happen the next time.

Memory on the point of taking form, it'll be repeated again, you must be the one who gives in and lets it drift, it's going to challenge you, completely take you over.

What business do I have dragging a dream from oblivion, stirring up a buried memory, they're not my orders, to confront the memory head on, to imagine it as a body made up of an image and words, to battle with its words, invent more of them so that they can absorb the others, dull their cutting edge, make the moans die out, the yells.

Mustn't mistake the target, roam in the wrong direction through this furniture traffic, silent commotion in the corridor, rooms doomed to refurbishment, or recycled for the newcomers filling the floor, struck by what you might call bad luck.

Maximum clutter, I step over various objects abandoned here any which way, progress restricted, arrested by packed obstructions, wood of every sort, polished or painted, varnished, lacquered, slats and branches, bark, stalks, and roots.

Straight and twisted boles, dense and thick undergrowth.

The light grows imperceptibly in the impassable passage, dawn light on the muddy path, those on patrol clearing a way through the forest, stealthily parting the branches.

I go on ahead to survey the obstacle, listening out for creaking sounds, the rustlings of the morning in that great mass of vegetation, raise my hand here and there to stop them for a moment, trying to catch the other who's also on his guard.

He's on his guard, I sense it, locked into the mindset of a private battle, he who's searching for me has it easier, it's in vain that he was appointed a courtesan to sap his strength, she brings him messages, who gives them to her?

That's what they say, she would instruct him as well on new subjects and ways of thinking, of linking words to things, or of words that set them apart.

To learn these words, recite them, tame them.

To make use of them.

Pale stains between the branches, blank spaces, pruning in the undergrowth, several more steps and the crater is at our feet, a missile that night had ripped the ground open, a pond at the bottom of the hole, blackish waters.

The ring of the forest around, stigmatized by this new cross, this is only a breach, a new twist in the plan, it's the same for him too, certainly, for the one slipping between the branches on the opposite edge of the hole, a wolf perhaps.

A stag halted in its tracks by the muddy excavation, bowed antlers hiding its body.

Or a wild boar, the herd wouldn't be far off.

There is no herd this morning, the beast is alone and its fleece appears flickering between the pine trunks, advancing with resolute steps around the perimeter of the crater, we advance in the same direction, cautious.

Diametric distance beneath the dawn's rays.

I said to my men, those in the vanguard, those at the front, those I had gathered in town before the attack and who were the ones closest to me, fuelled by the same passion, I told them to stay there, not to go any further, not to intervene, I have a score to settle, a rendezvous if you will, leave me to it.

A score between my shadow and the one that's approaching me, closing in on me for the last few minutes, and the two shadows combined and intersected, stacked up and shifted in confused lines, denial of awareness.

Then, I ran in the opposite direction and rushed toward the stretched shadow of the beast by the slope of the shrubbery.

Did I think myself capable of that? moment, movement of violent joy, experienced for so long now in dreams, those I remembered, those I forgot, movement of an enduring force held in check for so long.

Confrontation deferred, hidden in subterfuge by the nature of the terrain, the face-to-face a long time coming, it needed to be finished with.

The scene deserves to be confronted today, the enigmatic return to the aged body, the passage must be taken on each time in a wave, a vision, a trance still living.

I was looking for you, says the Quartermaster standing between two piles of clutter, motionless, voice calm, patient, as if he'd been there a good while, from the very start of the episode, and had hesitated a long time before saying anything.

You weren't in your room, I have something to show you, this way, it's shorter, you've almost gone the whole way around, it'll be easier for you after a while.

I had been very close to the last turning point, you could see the reception from there, he went ahead of me, was already stepping aside in order to let me in.

On the big table, a mauve file, he opened it briefly and I saw what looked like rough outlines, or photographs, newspaper clippings as well no doubt.

He took out the document on top, handed it to me, miniature color photo, a little blurred, a high mountain in the background, the snow, the earth red in between, and him in the center, Wild, sitting on a rock, weapon in hand.

I'm there to his left, standing, rifle slung over my shoulder, taking a photo perhaps, you can't see very clearly.

That was in Africa, wasn't it? there's nothing on the back.

I remained silent, giving back the picture, going back through the door, he understood his mistake straight away, handing it to me.

Shouldn't be taken by surprise, in my state, shouldn't be rushed.

Pain, the gradual alleviation isn't a given, to see every image, to work on each of them, one by one, detach yourself from it after assimilating it, neutralize its blast.

Kill it.

Action of words on the flesh of illness, to hound the words that upset me, find new words to upset me.

I followed the corridor, found myself in my room, I was going to say my bedroom, that word is soothing, it would be good to sleep here.

Shaken by the brief scene, somewhat disappointed in the Quartermaster's ill-conceived move, might have suspected it all the same, did he want to cut corners?

Psychology to be reviewed, go over the manual again.

An eye on the pages, the overly sharpened pencil, incomplete movement toward the white paper, it's no use writing when emotional, I had the time to let it fade and recompose it, as sharp and free as it would be, all present, so he could read it whenever he wanted afterward.

Click of the time switch, I fall into the armchair with its old-fashioned articulation, open it out further, close my eyes.

The image is there behind my eyelids, scaled down on the retina in black and white, simplified, the two silhouettes turned toward one another on the rocky spur, the sparkle of snow.

It's displaced a little, am I imagining that, toward the left, come a long way from when it was taken and fixed, the expedition there, shady exploits overseas, what did we intend to do in those places?

Desire for exile, standing back after the war, other values, other ideas, to leave on discovery again.

On reconnaissance.

My appearance always a bit awkward, stiff movements inside my head, result of tradition in my social background, artificial turns of phrase, a fear of letting go that was falsely considered prudishness, this constraint of self had been imposed since birth, sometimes limiting my speech.

His profile clear still between eyelids and retina, the snapshot endures, tracks the actor of the silent film, no special effects, the mechanism of the eye operates, forces me to look.

Hair in abundant curls on his shoulders, the nose short and thick, those teeth too long between the large lips, supple body broken in from childhood to the running and hazards of rock, the ripples of the desert, the nearness of beasts and wild grasses.

Instructed in solitude and feared by shepherds, by hunters.

They used to say.

They still say, echoes of legend, partners in the legend, he and I, summed up by stories, truncated words, inaccurate words making the paradoxical line tasteless or sublime, inconceivable on paper, the waves, the screens.

Didn't think of him under the nib.

Withdrawal here, respite, time of coming back to life, the surrounding of these miserable materials helps to properly focus the tragedy, to clearly determine what's at stake and make it understood, the truth of the line broken by death.

Nothing else in view otherwise, no diversion, detour.

A success, all in all.

Those footsteps in the corridor, almost timorous, on tiptoes, not those belonging to the movers in the corridor, presumably here to take away the clutter over in the other wing of the building, I was busy there for a while, I think.

An afflicted soul serving his time, moving about furtively from one door to the next, looking for a room, seeing images again like I do, all resonant at present, equal in emotion, of the same value, whatever the scenes may have been.

Turns the doorknob, pushes the swinging door, his profile against the light, he sees nothing but darkness outside his shadow on the floor in the pale pool of light.

What is he looking at, doesn't see me, he gets bored, pulls the door toward him.

I hadn't closed the door, no longer a key in the door, he must have taken the key with him, the key was no longer here beforehand, what's going on with the keys?

In the corridor, with these footsteps? multiplying, inspectors or controllers, experts or visitors.

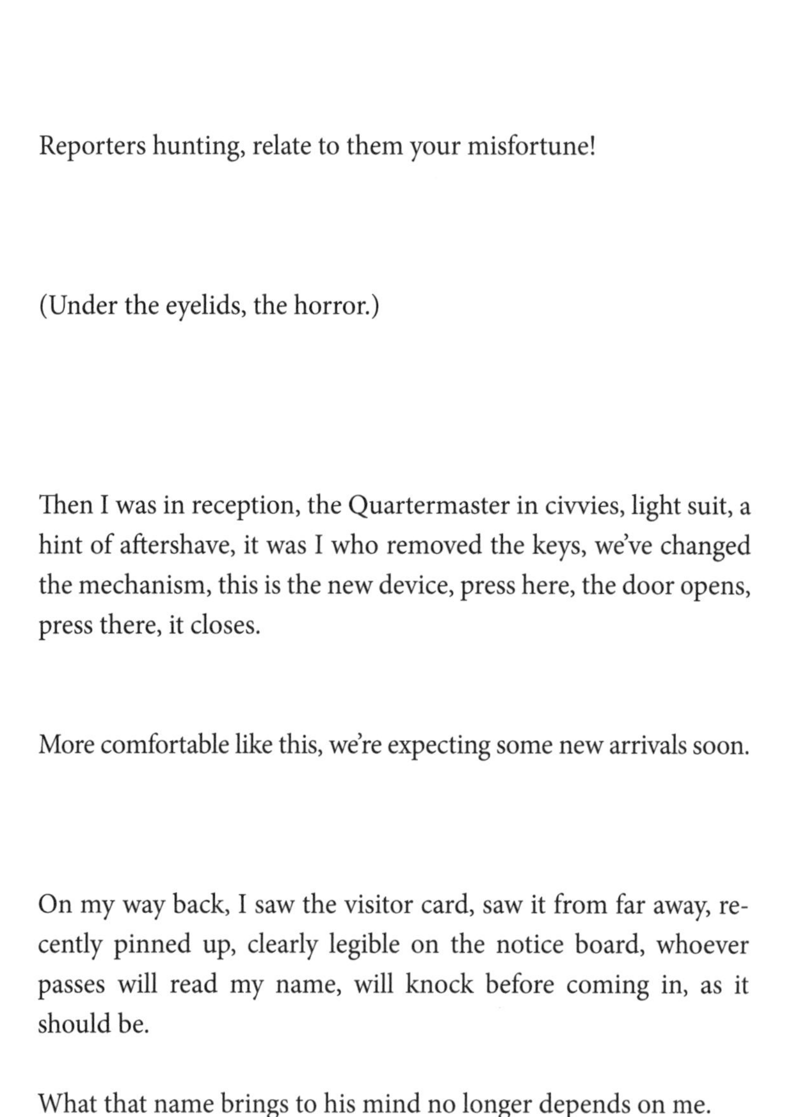

Reporters hunting, relate to them your misfortune!

(Under the eyelids, the horror.)

Then I was in reception, the Quartermaster in civvies, light suit, a hint of aftershave, it was I who removed the keys, we've changed the mechanism, this is the new device, press here, the door opens, press there, it closes.

More comfortable like this, we're expecting some new arrivals soon.

On my way back, I saw the visitor card, saw it from far away, recently pinned up, clearly legible on the notice board, whoever passes will read my name, will knock before coming in, as it should be.

What that name brings to his mind no longer depends on me.

Will remind him of nothing whatsoever no doubt.

Welt, some would say, others *Werk*, by mistake, through confusion, but *Wert* is my name.

That no longer depends on Wild, Wild isn't here to shout my name on catching sight of me, then hurrying forward.

Isn't here anymore to link my name to his, our names will survive, who knows, cited by the Ancients, mouth to ear, oral traditions, soon recorded on papyrus or clay, our exploits magnified, outrageous legends.

I had to keep from drowsing, to set aside my thoughts, staring at the dark, every knock startling me, I pressed the button and the Quartermaster burst in, crumpled lightweight suit, lit up, without ceremony went straight to the table, leafed through the scrawled pages.

Read them rapidly or pretended to, simply glanced through, put them back in order, reclassified them in the file.

Seemed satisfied, said well done with the fighting, very good, the fighting was important, the duel in the forest.

Remained a moment at the door, turned toward me, embarrassed, nose to the ground, was going to say something important about the management of the institution, its functioning or foundation, its purpose, or so it seemed to me.

Thought better of it, didn't breathe a word, nodded his head, slipped away.

I pressed the other button and the door locked, it was dark again, why come here, in a whirlwind, he's pressed for time perhaps, what's he planning?

What could happen here that would disrupt the ordinariness of things happening over and over again and taken in hand by the subject, supported and worked on through and through, montage in a loop, actions frozen, magic lantern to besiege and exhaust the patient, surviving bearer of ruined affection, actor and witness, will be nothing but a witness later, will no longer bear anything.

To appear here in the half-light of the room that's oh-so-very-peaceful to the recluse trying to find peace, the way of appeasement, of rupture with the lost object!

Room of destinies, reading the past afresh from the tablets.

Steel and spearheads in the flesh, in the clay as well, tattoo of skin, of stone.

Letter stamped, carved clean into the tissue, almost ingrained, a millennium cut in heavily, indelibly.

Icon given its due, vain promise.

I engrave my tablet, my own past, my old past, scribe by trade, plagiarist or crude apprentice, amateur striking the pose.

Of some profession all the same, intoxicated early on by verb and grammar, syntax rebelling in my head, effervescent, bursting the bubble.

Wild never had this problem, whatever I taught him of those things, words and things, was simply useful to him, was ordinary in fact, another grammar tensed his muscles.

The words were only for naming the instinct lodged in him by the savagery of the savannah, for refining it, stimulating it further.

Instinct forged by breath and cries, then by words.

Me, stimulated by words, on a quest for the breath outside the city of the war, spread out beyond the norm, on a quest for an alternative to breath.

Raising a little troop among the members of my clan, putting off escape from the circle of birth, late, fallen from the sky and as such, greeted with sudden determination, slightly suspect.

Shots from outside, urgent call.

Inexperienced infantry ill-equipped on the heights, the hunted hunting the unseen, unheard enemy, rushing through the night and giving up at dawn, skirmishes cut short, frustration of patrolling in an unfamiliar zone littered with decoys.

That region beyond, where we can't go, the huge forest to the north, the enemy's seeded it with redoubts and reduits, there's a fortress in the center, a runway for the planes dusting the towns and plains with bombs.

Primary force launching raids and attacks, harrying the convoys, burning hamlets and farms.

We're there in the snow, the wind, murmur of Wild on the wind.

Is this how I would have described the duel?

What status should I give, in this confined space, to the memory of actions planned or committed, of deployments postponed or acted upon, of words thought, of words written in the mind or on a sheet of paper?

I remember having planned to write it down, having imagined, dreamed it, did I really describe it then, rather than simply dreaming of doing so?

But the page of the duel appears prominently on the table, the Quartermaster left it there, didn't put it away with the others in the file, it would be the most recent no doubt.

Left it so I'd remind myself of it or really read it or reread it, bring back to mind the exact circumstances, the truth of the event.

I can read it like this, as though someone else had written it, had lived the scene or questioned the witnesses, made an ordinary testimony of the rumor, of the face-to-face and of the fight.

Forcing his way through the undergrowth in one bound, swooping down on me, my hearing less sharp, deprived of signs to decipher in the silence of the flawlessly maintained approach on both sides of this game of hide and seek, hand-to-hand combat fierce from the first instant, mobilizing mind and heart, muscles and nerves, hiding the surrounding decor from our eyes, we were rolling on the rocks in conjunction with feints and attacks, picking ourselves up we'd collide with branches, the strong trunks of the pines in the path of the brawl.

Did I hear our shouts in the confused entanglement of movements as we sized one another up, gauged each other's strength, straining to breaking point, recoiling, uncoordinated maneuvers, moving very slowly at times in order to catch our breaths, both of us needing the break?

After a time that only the men in my troop could estimate, standing to one side watching and not intervening, just as I'd instructed, respecting orders even at the worst moments, we were suddenly facing one another and he was no longer attacking, watching me seemingly surprised, his expression amused.

Possible, yes, plausible testimony, it was certainly necessary to choose, to filter, link together, but where did the essence of it lie?

I didn't speak of blows received, of the weight of those blows that would stun you and make you lose your nerve, of the weight of the blows dealt, delivered where it would hurt most, by guesswork often if not entirely blindly, blows missed and thrown again, missed again.

Blows for nothing, into the void.

He was no longer attacking, he laughed and I saw his face, the whole of his face revealed in the shifting light of his eyes, going from light gray to dark purple, to blue suddenly, an incredible pale blue.

His other features stood out thanks to his gaze, thanks to the intensity of his eyes, you couldn't pick them out except on the periphery as under a light veil obscuring their shapes, his nose was short, flat, forehead narrow, deeply wrinkled, his mouth hard.

The mane of blond curls gave his head a flowing, vague effeminacy.

Standing straight and stepping aside a little, surprised, by my courage no doubt or my unexpected resistance, though less surprised than I, the educated one, the libertine treating himself to words and adventures, scholar experienced in other battles, not to these impromptu ones in some goddamned forest.

Or he spared me, could at any moment have knocked me out and struck me down with a definitive blow, his arm held back, he thought better of it.

Fell.

Reached out to me and our hands joined, our bodies clasped in an embrace unequivocally deciding the result of our contest, my men came up and cheered us, carried us off in triumph.

I was stunned, that was exactly the idea which had motivated me in going to war, so that was the idea then, vague design, I'd feel it without putting any faith in it, it would show on the surface, then flit away, would return to trouble my nights, make me speak of it.

To confront the one about whom the talk in town was becoming more and more exaggerated, veiled terms told of the savagery of his name, of his bestial state and lack of education, of his flamboyant illiteracy.

The girl is never far away, the whore paid to settle him down, she introduced him to the rules of language as well, taught him about the surrounding world, and he developed quickly, far cleverer than she was.

Told him my name, about my past, my reputation, the possibility of a challenge was planted in his mind, desire for battle and reconciliation, amity, how did she know?

She lingers here, follows us everywhere, I sense her close by, cunning escort somewhere in the vicinity, has an effect on him still, perhaps, and he slips away, lets me down.

Could have made contact with my men, plotted the whole thing? Fair's fair, takes one to know one.

Naive and cunning alike, we all celebrated the moment, on the trail back to the camp Wild took me aside, whispered in my ear that he knew the way to the fort, knew how to bring down its fortifications.

How to get through the maze and mine the towers.

Initial gesture of friendship, an aside offered in confidence, unexpected, others followed, significant threads in the fabric of memory, they crop up again unexpectedly, all features mingled, superimposed, only the locations vary.

Wild to my left takes my arm, his lips close to my ear whisper what he's just learned or understood or has known for a long time and didn't dare say, and that will alter the stakes completely.

Will alter the facts of the problem, which keeps us on edge, mobilizes all our competence and strength.

Recurrent impulsion reinforcing our pact, he comes to me, eyes bright, whispers those words of his or the words of a message passed to him through betrayal or the bitterness of rejection, he knows the price of baseness.

That was one time in the mountains from the photo of Africa, he could have shouted the words, declaimed them, roared, we were alone, not a soul around, he appeared suddenly, silently, muffling his step, whispering the barbaric name of the gorge where we should stage our ambush.

In his element in those parts, the enemy looks like him, as boorish and beaten-up as he is.

Wild left his soul in that country, his body was soon struck by an abrupt and still unnamed sickness.

Only his body was here, heaped with honors.

These words as ineffective in holding back emotion as they were at preventing it from rising up in the first place, what words can I set down to neutralize it, control it, put it away?

In the room, still seated at the table in the dark setting lines on paper, trying to reread them, the words pouring out with that old proficiency acquired during childhood or at birth, distant ancestry, skill that isn't enough to exhaust the voice completely, the continuous flow of terms with rhyming and onomatopoeic endings, other things are mixed in there, conveyed, which are disregarded by clear speech, it pretends to disregard, and conceals it badly.

Fixation with that which is ephemeral, the voice emblematic of the ephemeral, a particular process gradually grinds it down, erases it utterly, the voice deprived of feature from the very beginning.

Your word all the more elusive because it will be the right word, in it shines the fragile spark, a brilliance lights it up at the instant of setting it down and of losing it.

Such a word, effectively passed into the ethereal permanence of this record, or had already disappeared, all these things that were understood had already disappeared, lifeless for a long time now.

To go on understanding the words that no longer exist to be understood.

Head inundated by words in the darkness, bent in weariness over the table, forehead fallen on the paper, staring at the pages.

Only my body here, my mind in that distant country of our adventures, tournament of fire in the darkness.

My ear listening for knocks, for steps in the corridor that it would be alone in perceiving, an ineffective synapse prevents me from hearing them.

Noise, who's moving, would move in, what phantom?

They're certainly of flesh and bone, the bodies moving around in search of the place assigned to them, for meditation and regaining control, their secret place of treatment.

From behind the door I follow the comings and goings, the great silence reigning in this institution, for as long as I've been here at least, makes the movement seem excessive to me; no doubt it's only one or two residents, or maybe only two or three bustling about.

Hand on the door handle, the door swings open by itself, a young man passes, his head doesn't turn, he sees nothing, hears nothing, what's in his head is from a crumbled world, he never leaves it.

I cross the threshold, watch him move away, going from one door to another from right to left deciphering the cards that have just been pinned up, doesn't find his name, turns at the corner, head stiff, indifferent to his surroundings.

Gripped by an image, not of his blackouts and flashbacks, of the omnipresent and the pathetic mark of boundless melancholy that's affected his entire life.

A disappearance, breakdown, or betrayal, presence vanishing before his eyes and his maniacal drift through the barely lit corridor that now closes up again.

Body forging along on its own, moving itself mechanically, only responsive to obstructions and changes of direction, was I like that at the very beginning?

I went as far as the corner, turned, didn't see the new arrival again, had he found his allocated place of seclusion and retreat?

Retraced my steps, read some names here and there, numbers on every door, Roman numerals in white chalk, haven't seen these numbers before.

On my door, the numeral *I*, wavy vertical stroke capping my name, I was the first then, in the new building I mean, I would have inaugurated it.

Broken it in, in sum.

The Boss was keeping an eye on me, worried I'd complain, I hadn't complained about anything, he was there to start things off, that's all, once reassured he handed things over.

I wasn't happy with this numeral, it didn't suggest anything of value to me, I ran to reception, they could have consulted me all the same, asked me my opinion, hadn't I chosen the room?

That's good, you're reacting, said the one sitting behind the table in front of a mass of files and who wasn't the Quartermaster, was older than him, as though he'd gotten thinner; had a goatee, a dark, worn suit, maroon bow tie on a white shirt, pince-nez.

A good sign, standing up for yourself, though you're not the first of course, first at the reopening if you will, after all the work we did, we totally renovated last year.

Numeral *I* purely indicative if you will, like the first person pronoun, without established connection with the one who signs, the signature itself without formal connection . . .

I'm here to inspect the works, advise the new arrivals, assess the progress of their texts, take note of their behavior, their diligence, I'm the Master in a manner of speaking.

Call me Master.

Very well, Master.

Someone who's grief-stricken as you are, as well known as you are, ought to be a model, you understood that quickly, the report I have here does you great credit.

Thank you, Master.

It's the Quartermaster who wrote it, he told me you used the reception office in the beginning, that wasn't regulation, but you made good use of it at least.

Wild wasn't regulation, wasn't civilized, even in distress, was in distress at the end, suffering from an unexplained sickness, he rebelled, hurled abuse, cursed fate.

Wild driven since birth, from wherever he had come, through what conspiracy, decreed from on high, treacherous cunning.

I'll see you once I'm done with these wretched papers, I've been promised an intern, thank the Lord, you can go now.

I returned to my room the long way around, the clutter had been removed, the way was clear, bumped into two new arrivals at the corner before my door, room numbers in hand, they were fumbling blindly, I wanted to help them, they seemed not to understand.

Returned in good form, happy, as if I hadn't been back to this room in years, I feel at ease here, feel connections here.

Door wide open, I hadn't closed it, nothing to take except the papers, which I can recreate, no one came in, why would they bother, this filing cabinet in the half-light perhaps, I'd lost sight of it, its jammed drawers that no longer slide open, what's in there, brushes, dust?

The idea gained ground, I would be able to leave soon, but you leave when you want, who exactly is keeping you here? you can go immediately if that makes you happy, the Master will cross out your name, make you sign the register, good-bye, have a good day!

You know very well you can't leave yet, it's difficult for you to say that, you have to be forced, to open the breach wide and to fill it in.

Light extinguished, I make my way to the armchair, these hands no longer blindly feeling their way in the dark, three sidelong steps to the right and here I am sitting down, reclining soon enough, this seat softer than it appears, it's molded to my body.

Knew my way henceforth in this confined cubbyhole, this attic of memories and sensations engraved into the body, deeply set images so slow to fade, a compact and closed world outside all chronology, no sequence, no flashes, no bolts of lightning.

Posture conducive to calming down and taking a step back from things, you're the one reflecting, weighing, he followed the path, was pushed along the path.

As soon as the pact was sealed and the secret of the fort was delivered to my ear, we broke camp of our own initiative in the evening after discussing supplies and tactics.

A final glance at the lights of the town, at the patchwork of plots of low country land, thick hedges, clusters of reeds in the distance to the south.

Me in the lead on the route we knew well, gateway to the forest, he took the lead shortly afterward on a path whose twists and turns had put us off many times, overwhelmed us even, prisoners of a web of brambles.

Wild made light work of the traps, both nature's traps and those of the forest raiders, always the first to pause in his step, sensing the movements of an animal, narrowly skirting patrols.

Sometimes, on coming out of a cluster of trees, we'd emerge into a clearing where signs of combat could be seen, who could have sprung out here or there from the half-light and come face-to-face in the light, old signs, muskets, swords and culverins, broken spears?

Antique weaponry, striating the ground with bloody signs.

Stages of the journey slow at night, the big helicopters don't fly at night, searchlights ineffectual at flushing out men and animals in the undergrowth, they take off at dawn on their patrols, and the bombers over the plane, volleying the paths.

A heavy storm in the forest under the tremendous roar, arrows with phosphorus points stick slantways in the loose soil, crackle, go up in flames, one lands between my feet, silent, sudden, sets fire to me, the fire walks with me.

Incendiary pencils.

That was the other dream, also premonitory, it comes back to me in one go.

That dream, and the first heralding the encounter, his bursting into the field of childhood speculations or of age-old, endless cogitating, again he had a primeval constitution, evolved primitive, the long-awaited friend, sensed in a dream.

Twenty men around me in the forest and this disheveled guide who appeared from the undergrowth, the first ones wonder, coming from the world of cities, provided with too many conjectures, as for Wild, he only knows how to make a path, to drink from a pool of water, knows only sky and the scent of the winds, sounds from the steppe, silence of footfalls.

Profound silence, primordial, it will sweep up the leftovers of this drama, the dregs of sentiment, the remains of the storm.

I didn't sleep for even a moment, how could one sleep in this place of contemplation and retreat, the relaxation of the mind is not that of the body in any matter requiring at the least tension and mental strain, diligence, constraint.

To the point of rupture and disconnection, of every memory, of every object, no more stabbing pains, no more laments, a touch of irony will weaken the connection.

One day to your surprise the connection will be severed.

Wild was popular, what deliverance did the soldiers expect from him? I wasn't the only one expecting something.

Soldiers of solitude, we'll battle, love, procreate.

To dust we'll return.

The footsteps continued, increased in number, but no voice, no glances exchanged or bodies passing one another, I hear a door slam shut, slamming in my ear, a stock of minor noises recalling the time before the disaster.

Door half open, from my rudimentary divan I catch the eclipses of light in the visible section of corridor, they succeed one another, no novice pushes the swing door, or even pauses, takes the time to read the name, my name printed small, capitals agreed upon in the code as developed by the civilized city-dwellers, urbanities of the good old days.

Had they been given the map of the floor so they could rush along directly now, neither stopping nor hesitating, until they reached the dwelling awaiting them, similar to mine probably, chair and table and divan?

Bewildered sleepwalkers deprived of their lovers or friends, the emotional rupture marking their flesh, an excessive tear marking their skin.

Silence of the nonbelievers, withdrawn into their new speechlessness, such a long time alone.

I thought it was necessary to speak, they told me to express myself, to shout and act out, that would make me feel better, would make the sorrow bearable, there's no communication here between housemates, inmates of distress cloistered in our cabins of rationed light, strictly measured into equal slots of brightness, to be turned on as required in a disillusioned, disappointing, insistent way.

Little room for speech here where the mute voice allows you to feel the extent of the pain, it causes it to circulate, to revolve, leads it along and puts it in play; it takes so much attention to listen to that voice that the suppressed throat loses its resilience, becomes incapable of performing.

Won't the words measure up? they do in the mute voice, the phonic mechanism no longer responds, is jammed or has broken, waits in its wrecked state for the taste for speech to return.

The joy of uttering a sound, of yelling and murmuring, making oneself heard, hearing oneself shout, mumble, whisper, stammer the rest of what he has to say.

The sense follows, if it can, if the sense can be saved.

On its unbroken surface, the shape like a net will cast itself, its shadow will reveal the substance of each thing.

Three steps in front of me, the huge demon with his curly mane in his greatcoat of bear skin, which that ancient girl, prostitute of swamps and floods, must have cut, tacked, and sewn for him.

Authenticating the landmarks picked up on the wooded footpaths during the time of his animal childhood, sees the dangers in them now, scavenger hunt revealing the village or casemate, such a monstrous creature made in the heart of the forest.

Halting the small, modern, civilized detachment with a raise of his eyebrow, starting it back en route with a nod of his head, link or living symbol of our rallying for the same cause despite our differences.

Delighted fascination of the young bourgeois elite for the barely civilized scourer of the bush, half-naked, not at all civilized, his dumbfounded curiosity about their well-looked-after, polished faces, and the city dialects, words and turns of phrase he's not long picking up and handling with unsophisticated humor, uncomplicated enjoyment.

Everything works itself out between them quickly, one hour suffices for Wild to exert a stable influence on my men, imposing his skill, stamina, and cleverness on them.

Between us there is no dominance, automatic mutual respect, we were practicing it without thinking about it even before knowing one another.

That's how it happened, I'm not embellishing, we cut along at a rapid, cadenced pace with evening fallen on the undergrowth, we remained quiet, rifle or sub-machine guns in hand, he with his axe at his belt, hadn't made use of it yet.

How does he manage to direct his steps in the black night, we leave it to him, instinctively, will he lead us into the tiger's den some night?

Black-Heads in the ancient forest, or it seems ancient to us, launched on an expedition, a blind raid, vivid awareness of what's at stake, the secret of the path is revealed to us little by little, we earn it, a matter of courage, of awakening.

A wink in my direction here, watch your feet, message given quickly.

Wild the Fearless, journey in six stages, nights and bivouacs and sentinels posted, snow hardened on the warpath, strong winds, each one dreamed of his part.

Always a glint in Wild's eyes in the absolute darkness, me, Wert, alerted by an old expression, come back for the thousandth time to the course of a journey I now risk relating or writing, later on, closed up willingly in this cell.

If the world no longer pays you any attention, no longer grants you wind or sun, color, smell, then come here, shut yourself up here, what you had to lose is already lost, everything meaningful in this world lost.

Do as I do, here all luster is lost, all luminescence, taste and desire are no more, an absence of attraction same as outside, but more radical, more bearable too, at least you can probe this void, ponder it, maybe fill it up one day.

I raise my eyelids, no beam under the door anymore, no key under my hand anymore, the door opens however, I hear it swing and the light attacks, the Master is there, framed on a dark background, comes through the doorway.

Excuse me, I wanted to reassure you, there's a power failure in the halls, I have a double of the keys.

I'm going from room to room, it's part of my job, the new arrivals are shaken, handling it badly.

If I'm disturbing you, tell me, would you mind if I sat down?

The Master is there, isn't looking at me, what is he looking at in this outdated enclosure painted a dark, peeling brown, what on earth did they renovate on this floor last year, his performance of attendance drags on, doesn't bother me, perhaps he'll say something at the end but the time-switch locks with a click after a moment and the corridor appears completely dark, a ghost of gray light from the direction of reception after some time.

To get up would not have been favorably received, I don't want to offend, he visited me as promised but I can't see him, or even discern the outline of his body, and I'm a little surprised, the eye always ends up detecting some presence.

It only sees the absence of a human shape in front of the table where I scrawl, the table is only there by memory, and the jammed filing cabinet where I would have been able, in jest, to put my pages in order.

This room is for contemplation, haven't I contemplated enough, where does a contemplation dealing only with brooding lead, contemplating itself and managing without producing or bringing to a close or transforming into something new the brooded-over unhappiness, if not to say despair, a word that the one contemplating his own past never really liked?

Could say breaking point, misery, but I am no fonder of these narcissistic and darkly appealing words.

To suppress unhappiness and get back to the word that would express its opposite, if the richness of our vocabulary still prevailed?

Perhaps it's the Master who leads my contemplation along, manipulates it, or maybe he's having the same thought by chance at this moment and there's some kind of silent transmission going on, across a short distance to be sure, but a transmission all the same.

The sudden glare in the corridor like intense floodlighting reveals the absence of the Master, not even the afterglow of his body on the dull, cracked brown of the wall, but this is too much to demand of an already distant perception.

Was he here? came in, spoke, excused himself, explained himself, sat down on the chair.

Slid a note into the file, typed, the note shocks me.

You left him alone at the end, we know, he complained about it.

One typed line on a piece of paper inserted by a nimble hand in the dark, left as though by accident, surreptitious, anonymous.

What business is it of his and what does he know of him, of my men, of what Wild said, didn't say, of what I should have done, shouldn't have done?

To judge another, judge his actions, his words, who does he think he is?

Reception occupied but the Quartermaster wasn't there, wasn't sitting there, I'd angrily burst in again, calmed down in a flash, the new guy at the desk watched me without expression, I wasn't an object of curiosity for him, or concern, he stared at me without really considering me, his eye staring through me fixed on something I could feel, imagining me as an abstract drawing, invisible.

A pencil in hand, which hadn't yet written anything, would write little here if he wrote at all before migrating to other parts, lower down again, crossing the corridor and finding refuge there.

In his thirties, incredulous expression, didn't seem embarrassed that I was watching him.

It was I who broke the contact, the non-reciprocal connection, with a loss, there had been contact, from me to him, my attention had been held.

I came back along the other corridor, the long way around, surprised by having been affected by someone other than me, by something other than me, or that was nothing but a reflex from the past, carried forward secretly, differed without apparent motive in a place where nothing was allowed to be foreseen.

I was almost running, fleeing my look, to forget it as fast as possible.

Went back to my room, paced back and forth between filing cabinet and armchair, a little agitated, questioning myself, would I have ever found myself over the course of time, at a certain time, in a situation of this kind, marked by these poorly defined relationships, sporadic, lax?

At that moment, I was sure of it, and no, I had never known such a situation, prisoner of a specialized refuge and free to leave it, to head off when I wanted, certain, nevertheless, that my destiny was at stake, without really understanding why, here in the half-light.

The note on the table beside the file like an eye, taunting, those words that leave me stunned, my body heaves, bearing those words.

Rumor, what Wild thought of rumors, the roar of his laughter used to panic the birds, there were all sorts of little birds in the fig trees, in the walnuts, the olives, large birds in the caves, on the rock ledges, jackdaws, vultures, huddled up in their hideouts, wrapped within the swirls of the rock.

Our detachment ventured along mule tracks over a complicated and hazardous terrain, where the enemy who was ravaging the country was free to lay his ambush.

Furious bull, the name given by Wild to the one whose presence he had quickly learned to detect, he let him get away, sure of having him in the end, the man was surprising, devious, his strength superhuman, knew every hideaway, gorge, pass, or crevasse in the creases of the mountain, what an idea to try to look for him up there, and humiliate him, subdue him.

To hunt down his men, arrows and shells, muskets from another age exploding in your hands, burning the bone, those old village rifles.

Fury of the dissenter, rousing his clan, sewing terror among neighboring tribes, the invader is only a pretext in this story, it stems from intrigue between the country's chiefs, revenge they say, God knows for what.

Massive silhouette in the heavy, hooded coat of brown wool appearing suddenly here and there on the ridges, archetypal figure from fairy tales, a brigand, was much more than a brigand though, had been through skirmishes and sporadic assaults, the reality of an oppression that wasn't only that of the bushman, but of his friend too, his companion in this crusade.

Neither tanks nor planes in this adventure, no explosives or hails of bullets, it was a different war, fought with the same tactics as in the ancient forest, by both sides this time.

The men in the squadron followed as best they could, ready to play their part but always outrun, caught in the ripped up earth, ill-equipped for this old-style, outdated sort of campaign.

We flushed him out alone, he was foaming at the mouth, it took both of us, two strong young men to bring him down and have him at our mercy, Wild grabbed him by the nape of his neck and twisted his arms back, I plunged the cutlass into his throat in the end.

What whore was peering at us through the foliage?

Our hands washed in the torrent, we had waited for the others and returned to the plain, did our best to celebrate the outcome of the fray.

Great moments, the simplified image clear, the gestures fixed over time, little color.

No sound, the sound is in the gaze.

During this victory ritual, the signs of exultation seen so often on Wild's face were absent, the usual outpouring, without boasting, without vanity, a childlike joy.

His expression clouded over, in hindsight worried, he didn't want to talk, gave a wound as his reason, didn't identify it however, his excessive drinking was a sign of long-drawn-out suffering.

What was worrying him, if there were worries, he didn't let on, he had every reason to be satisfied that night.

He had a dream in the morning, the Ancients of the country surrounded him, holding council, I saw in it a source of hope and health, he read in it that the end was near.

He felt his heart falter, after twelve days an unknown figure took shape before his eyes, once sensed, it was always there, very close by, and it overpowered his expression.

Convulsed grin never seen before, the mark of inevitability hanging over every feature of his face, youth fleeing, deserting his skin, his eye.

Looked at me, held it against me for having thought of inevitability, this word like a farewell, I abandoned him, left him alone.

Could see the prayers behind his eyes, my friend continues to live, is going to continue to live for a long time.

To take his hand, so that my youth might save his blood from emptying out.

To see that horror replayed again between four badly built, badly painted, badly cleaned walls, that terror.

I was there observing what becomes of the body when the soul leaves it, you knew that I was going to be alone, you weren't alone yet, the ghost hadn't yet taken shape, what were you complaining about?

Endlessly inseparable, a few more moments to talk about a connection that belongs to the past.

Past always there, already filing away each moment, pared down before it's even happened.

Already past before being born, is that life without end?

Head between my arms on the table and the blank pages, fear of going back again to that place where my blood ran cold one day outside of time like all the other days.

It wasn't so long ago.

Explosion of grief stretched out and spread over centuries, years of stabbing heartache, months and weeks, nights and days of sorrow.

All that with life still going on!

Pressing on the button of the miniscule device, I opened the door abruptly.

I'm sorry, said the Master, I was listening, yes, you seemed to be ranting, shouting, it was impressive, believe me!

And he added, I didn't want to put you into this state, I was tactless.

Moved forward nimbly toward the table, helped himself to the note, stuck it in his pocket.

At least you were shaken, that's not a bad thing in itself, these shocks are salutary, in small doses.

I didn't hold it against him, he was right no doubt, I had made some progress according to him, he proposed there and then that I widen my domain.

Without waiting for my reply, moved the armchair toward the table, revealed a small door that I hadn't noticed before, the partition was covered in old, flowery wallpaper, peeling off a little everywhere, frayed, dismal.

The same magic key, electronic quite simply, opened this door long since blocked, the door slowly swung open, without creaking or sending up a cloud of dust, revealed a room similar to mine, smaller at first glance, without table or chair, a moth-eaten camp bed in place of the armchair.

You'll be able to rest better this way, breathe better too, and, moreover, your field of action is extended.

To better find your way around, I'm leaving the light on permanently, as is your preference we hear.

Should I have thanked him, the main door was already closed behind the Master's back.

My perspective was indeed widening, stretched out on the camp bed in a corner that was situated, if the partition was pulled down, exactly opposite where the filing cabinet would be, I entertained myself with the illusion of having a suite at my disposal, being able to stroll from room to room warmed my heart.

No light in the new space, the light coming in from the old space was more than enough, what did I need light for here, no newspapers in any case, no books, would the Master suggest those to me?

Did I close my eyes, resting more comfortably like that than on the old armchair, I thought I could make out a vague glow on the ceiling, a higher ceiling than the one on the other floor.

The idea that I was beginning to see things more clearly in this business made me laugh a moment.

It was good to laugh, if only for a moment, I hadn't laughed furtively, but openly, without bitterness, without derision or reservation.

Surprising not to hear the neighbors more, what are they doing in their rooms, no longer pass by except with muffled tread, everyone seems settled in, why go out?

No noise above either, or below, only the floor of dismay was populated, the level of torment, what level, can't remember any more, the day when I came up here, how many levels, and when was that?

The day when I could no longer walk, could no longer wander around, far from headquarters in the poor district alongside the river, or roam as far as the city limits, going along the river, to come back to the city, oblivious of my surroundings.

To start again, along by the water, whole days, nights?

How many days, no way of counting the days, neither light from outside nor watch nor giant hourglass relentlessly emptied of its contents, to be turned over every morning, every week, all the months and years of sand.

Steps back and forth counting off the time passed to form a line with the fitted carpet, which was starting to become bare in places, the wooden floor unvarnished for centuries.

Prison term in these quarters, captured and concentrated, creeping between the walls, I devour it with contained steps over the expanse of days and nights whose alternation is entirely concealed.

Time shut away pouring from one wall to the other, becoming more dense and expanding according to the inexhaustible flux of the voice leading back to the time of former happiness.

Scattered, rarefied in the dross of words.

Time stretched out in the space stingily allotted to better frame the work phases.

All space some moments, all times at others, by measure of the path searching for the way out, dogged, scouring the pathetic steppe.

What is this country then, I didn't want to be born in this country, the fault is mine!

Time wending softly between the trees over beds of packed pine needles crunching underfoot, glimpses snatched between the trunks, edges of space on the skirted route that he alone knew.

What mechanisms favored these furrows of images, ancient engravings, not so old however, cushions of air between the large maps.

The uneven relief of nervures will become uneven circles of obliteration, extenuation of color, whitening.

To penetrate the forest that was like a sequence of colors, nocturnal arteries between fences of reeds, you couldn't see a thing, the instinct of the savannah man saved us from disaster.

Fighter planes high in the sky weaving lines of fumes, low-flying choppers disturbing the foliage, eagles and vultures gliding over the bivouac.

Patrol dogs, Wild let them come, cowed them I don't know how.

On the third leg we'd gained the peaks by the end of the night, ravine of loose stones between the cedars, cut our course.

The fervor deserted my blood, but about-face was impossible, I hesitated, lost my nerve, vertigo, he guided my step in the dips between rocks and stumps that barely stood out against the sky.

From the opposite ridge, the stronghold towered up in the distance the following day, ramparts crenulated against the white of the dawn.

We spent days in the winds of frost and dust, the flurries like hails of bullets though the weapons remained silent, my men had given up, only we two remained to wait for the whirlwind to abate.

I see myself on the other side of the partition covering the sheets with downstrokes and symbols punctuating the stream of words, why aren't I sitting in front of the table over there doing whatever is necessary to complete my report, under surveillance, that used to seem easy, maybe the Master is keeping track.

Up to him to tell me where I stand in my task, will I stay here my whole life, all the time which remains of my life; Wild is dead and I'm going to die, what we accomplished is fading, three or four shattered old tablets in a pit filled with the wind of the deserts, miracle if an enthusiast unearths them one day.

Puts their hand on them, frees the fragments of age-old detritus, exhumes the small, raised marks and exhausts himself trying to decipher them, dumbfounded by their strangeness alone.

No uncorrupted mark on them, nor any clever reader to scrutinize such a mark, do what he could to penetrate whatever secret he believes it might hold.

With what secret could the decay be penetrated, what unstoppable virus?

Have I talked about the camp bed? folding, flexible bed with a soft mattress, the well-stuffed pillow keeps my head raised to observe everything, so my sight extends as far as the filing cabinet over there on the right.

Spontaneous images, no need to force them, to evoke a particular scene, has it left its mark on you, coming through a weak or delicate chink in your armor? The scene will be replayed by itself, a word is enough leave this kind of mark on you, ringing out clearly and showing itself.

Slip of the tongue or restrained gesture repeated ad infinitum, not the strong and well-cast words, the noble gestures if there were any, chivalrous, no such words were ever enunciated, the actor would be disturbed, embarrassed, would find himself dubbing in new dialogue over the old.

The original, does it still exist, film reduced to dust?

Will this scene be replayed, this moment, will they often play over in the afterlife that's looming ahead?

The afterlife of time spent in these miserable premises being subjected to imposed flashbacks of the malevolent signs of those mornings of battle and promises of victory, all others blotted out, take them as they've become, blurred periphery of the image and contraction of duration, a feeling takes over your body during those flashbacks, and will remain intact.

To speak of battle, isolated as we were, did we still know what we were doing, furtively crossing over the moats paralyzed with frost under the scanty glow of the stars, Wild, sure-footed, was on his guard, searching for the right point in the wall, me stumbling along, slipping at every step, the case of explosives settled on my shoulders.

This small charge laid opposite the main one was a stroke of genius, they let themselves be fooled, the blast of the gunpowder flaring up into the sky like a missile, the monster reared up, his great body dismembered, burned to a cinder, leaping about trying to avoid the bursts of flame.

Deep darkness swooped down on the mountain.

Our steps signaled the withdrawal, the flaming snow blurred our tracks, face stained black, Wild turned around exultant in the noise echoing gradually through the forest, little by little, on the other side of the ravine, my incredulous men staring at the ruin, binoculars fixed to reddened eyes.

Final episode, already glorious in the annals, a poem would praise it, schoolchildren would learn it by heart.

Group photo in the archives, numbered, filed, with all those from the war.

And the whore lying in ambush was laughing.

We came back along the river, did the full tour of the country, taking our time, triumph we capitalized on day by day, wearing down in unhurried navigation, we let ourselves be looked after, in the towns the people cheered, from one shore to the other they shouted to us, a rumor grows, reaches the city.

Someone calls out here, with a guarded voice in the corridors, very close as well, on the other side of the partition, I stick my ear to the partition, listen.

Another ear listens, stuck to mine.

It's only a thin panel of wood, I slide it across quietly, the other is there looking at me, has moved back a little in the storage room, I make him out in the distant light from my lamp.

What surprises me, surprises him too perhaps, is the unusual layout of the storage room, an attic with curved sides, the roof steeply sloping, you'd think that the floor must narrow here, coming up against an obstacle, it ends abruptly, our floor must be the top floor as well.

Eye to eye, without surprise, without fear, he moves backward, away from me, as far as the door on the corridor side, he's left it open, came out accidentally into this corner, was expecting it as little as I was.

He's an Elder, the wrinkles attest to it and the jowls, the bald head, I thought I was the most senior, this meeting pleases me, I'm about to tell him but the corridor door slams shut, my panel slides back with a clatter.

I sit up in the bed, see the Master sitting at the table there.

You slept, that's excellent, so important for you to sleep, you're finally resting again after such a long period of sleeplessness.

I believe you may even have dreamed, the chart will reflect that, I'm keeping you up to date.

He slips away and I feel the partition, my hands flat on the partition, no panel, no sliding or aged inmate lost under the roof.

I must have slept, the store cupboard would be the place from the dream, I was almost touching its temporary occupant, I wanted to speak to him, hear the voice of a recluse, here from the very beginning, voluntarily or otherwise, so he might tell me about the history of this place, of the institution, the old story of unfortunates caught in a vice, the obsession with loss, the abandonment.

Steel chain, plaited ropes gripping my head, preventing it from moving, from relaxing, from thinking.

He must have wriggled out of it, I must have made him run away, I who made the dream made him move away from me, did he have nothing to say after all this time, the unfathomable length of time being awake, broken neither by sleep nor dream nor respite?

Yes, he was dreaming too, I wanted him to sleep and dream, to have someone with whom he could speak as well.

Why had he run away when I wanted him to speak, maybe I didn't want it enough.

Him behind the partition perceiving the noise I was making as I settled myself in the little room granted me by the Master for good behavior or something like that.

Not to mention the light being on permanently, according to my wishes of course.

Had the Master wished me to speak with the Elder who had lost his way in the dead-end under the attic? had he wanted me to sleep, simply, to keep this expressionless mask as a memory of this place, face inert, half-dead but living nonetheless.

I'll keep him in mind, will see him again, and he, wherever he might reside within my desire or that of the Master, will hear the noise I make on the other side of a partition, will listen to it with his ear glued to the wood or to the paper, will find himself face-to-face with the stranger or his double again in the afterlife of the ordeal.

What ghost from his past is haunting him, what powerful gaze is he incapable of erasing or dulling in his memory, has his time here likewise been regimented for him?

Is it the second time I'm saying the afterlife of the ordeal.

To take the step depends on me alone, I've said it a hundred times and a hundred times have remained, unfinished work in progress, to get to the bottom of things, not to lose one's nerve.

Sleep returned, I no longer thought of sleeping, have I ever thought of it since I've been here, came here, address known to everyone, no problem, I went in and sat at reception, opened the file and read the papers, got an idea of the case, attentive to the Boss's remarks.

Sleep would be the sign, resumption of the cycle of broken days, to live like before is no longer possible, the constraint of my obscure experience has cut off what was before, neutralized what went before.

How to live afterward?

I appreciated this bed instead of the old armchair, stale with the sweat of the Elders, got up without difficulty, found myself lighter, head freer, the vice released during the night perhaps, what else could've changed?

Went out for a walk, to stretch my legs, hardly anyone in the corridors, two youths stared at me, seemed distressed, eyes dull, it's me who's the Elder this morning.

Evening or morning, what to say anymore?

Came back to the apartment, sorted my papers, my filled pages, the others, the Master will do with them as he pleases, will burn them, frame them, note down expressions, will quote them in his manual or copy whichever of them into his personal diary.

I had felt well at this table, and sitting lopsided in the armchair, will have had good moments in this place, scribbling to punish the passage of time, so that time should slip by and drain away the misery of the rupture that chills me to the bone.

A last glance over the room, I put out the light as I pass the door, bolt the door with a sober electronic action.

Nobody at reception, perhaps the Master and his dream chart have slipped away, I place the key on the desk just in case, push open the door to the landing, leave this cruel place of retreat.

It was the top floor, I knew it.

Seven flights of stairs without remembering the climb, offices on the other floors and no noise, little light, tiling on the barely lit ground floor.

Distant voices in the street, the transom tells me that it's night time.

Full moon, and this long rectangle on the tiles, a void at my feet, I remain on the edge of the white stain that's spread on the tiles.

Then I go through the door, wordlessly admitted into the afterlife of grief.

II

Momentum

—the place

What good is it to have come this far just to turn back?

Or simply to remain here, to linger, to no longer move?

Neither in one direction nor the other.

To sit down on this rock and watch the dirty water spasmodically inundating the stones with its feeble waves.

Unremarkable shore, worn out by history, to follow it was exhausting, his eyes were disappointed to light on those crumbly cliffs, oakum grasses, shrubs with gray foliage leaning over a shore where no sand softened one's step.

Wert questions himself, feels himself waver, has flashes of doubt about his strength, about the validity of his itinerary, about his very purpose, even doubting his desire still, this black sea that swallows him.

Would have come this whole way and then retraced his steps again, would carry the desolation of a renouncement in his heart on the return journey, which would later double this unbearable bitterness.

Would return to his city sorrowful, would see sorrow in the eyes of his men, sarcasm in the eyes of the others.

Would submit to what everyone calls destiny.

Ought to have gone further south, through the mountains down south, convinces himself in his despair to follow an unattractive coast, the geographic negation of his quest.

It rains a lot, Wert only likes the rain when it's beating against the windowpanes, rain is connected in his mind to his dwelling place, takes him back there.

Someone spoke to him of a desert further on, further to the east, and of crossing it in order to join the one whose secret soothes his mind and makes him keep going, step by step, over the stones, the shingle, the absent sand.

How long ago his nocturnal flight seemed, the famous metropolis connecting landlocked seas and landmasses, golden in the morning, perceived as the real starting point.

How far distant those terribly slow trains moving over the tawny steppe that curved down toward the northern coast and its villages in the silted up channel bereft of sails.

This road extended from the track and he was carried along it by trucks and makeshift coaches over a plethora of ruts to a port, from which the only paths were the stone ones along the cliffs.

And Wert set off walking along the dreary shore, reflecting and deploring.

Wild, a phantom on the sleepy, motionless earth down below.

The thought like a blast breaking his momentum, if momentum can be used to describe such halting stages of a journey, and a repeated overlapping of monotonous days when the plan would lose its glimmer with every stride.

Fervent plan, desperate as it was, perhaps the mythical Ancestor is waiting for him there, meditating on time without end and on his perenniality, which was attested to in those ancient texts so strange to the eye and the ear.

Wert, in the prime of life, picks up a signal here and there all the same, his body senses the danger, awareness doesn't follow, still favors insouciance.

Mistakes the time as he searches for a reflection of the sky on the sea in the distance, or the wake of some sea creature to distract him from his route, sees only the high promontory to the east curving the shoreline.

Forges ahead, driven by his defiance, the question that occupies his mind is always there, every moment of his life remains, he is afflicted by loss and the unfairness of it, the disgrace in his eyes, under his eyes committed.

His feet refuse the last step, grisly demise, body stiff with no more breath, no more shocks, colors, flesh already rotten, corroding the memory.

Tainting the idea of face, the image of the hands, the eyes.

Evening has fallen over the wavelets and their meager backwash, stretched on the small bit of grass and the stones between two slopes, Wert knows that he's gone too far now, won't retrace his steps, without seeing it he's passed the point of no return during one of these recent days of fine rain.

Well equipped, strong, overdid it perhaps, his muscles are going numb, stiffened through nocturnal inaction.

Slept without intrigue, washed with still water.

Expeditions, duels, profusion on first awakening, all materials of the dream held on the verge of being represented, neither abstraction nor displacement, actors dismissed, the stage emptied.

Drowsy sleeper surprised suddenly by not having dreamed.

A morning without rain, pale in the dawn, on the shore below a fisherman is scraping the sides of his boat with a forked spade.

Repeated stridence of the maneuver, the non-dreamer gives a start, opens his eyes, sees the fisherman down below, is up in no time packing his things, haversack, kit.

Descends with cautious steps over the rocks crumbling in slabs as though abandoned to some never-ending disaster, some flowers in the hollows, withered narcissi, daisies, a type of lily of the valley.

The man hasn't heard the foreigner coming, turns around, young face, and his eyes have the seriousness of older people, the fixity of attention, the long patience.

Forked spade on his shoulder, he points out his boat, speaks in slow words, composed, you have to remove these creatures from time to time, to scrape, to scrape.

The boat is encrusted with cones, cowries, razor clams, barnacles, crustaceans.

With tower-backed shellfish.

Where are you trying to get to in that direction, stranger, you'll find nothing that way, find no one.

Nobody anymore.

Ah yes! Me, I'm here!

The others there at sea, in rough weather, all those fish dead, the poison.

Didn't seem in too much of a hurry to take up his work again, who's in a hurry on this deserted shore, the foreigner ought to be in one to find the right path.

The desert to the south, yes, you see the doubled peaks up there, follow the ravine straight ahead, climb as far as the top.

Wert took note of the reference points, he heads off toward the ravine and then that strident sound can be heard once more, echoed by the mountain, the movement of the forked spade on the side of the boat.

Some shells on the surrounding wall, surrounding the town.

Similar shapes revising the memory, structuring recollection.

At a given moment, the sun joins him, weakly, enough to color the rocks, raise contrast on the foliage, to enhance the monochromatic grayness of the landscape.

So he had drifted, knew that he was drifting and wasn't overly bothered by it, almost held it against the fisherman for having put him on the right track, the one his men had whispered about, age-old words spoken in one another's ear, a long tradition of urban orality, those really in the know ready and waiting, eager to erase.

At this moment he's crossing a difficult section, glazed with loose stones coughed up by storms over the ages, he loses his footing and is driven off course.

Is gaining altitude despite everything, regularly, still walking steadily, turns around from time to time, notices sails in the distance, spread motionless against the dark purple haze on the horizon.

Can still make out the fisherman and his boat, perceives a wave of the hand.

Beautiful play of light on the curls of the swell.

Thinks that his determination to leave was justifiable, couldn't stay in his native city living off of his anger, his grief, had to move, fly, travel a long way, and especially walk, walk a long way alone, would have left even without a destination, which came at the right time, who had even suggested it to him?

Dry torrent, a trickle of water, maybe there are pools between those large rocks further up, trout would be trapped up there and would turn, glazed with pink speckles.

Poplars on the banks, beech trees, ashes with suspect black spots, crumpled leaves, cracked, autumn is still a long way off.

Asphyxiated elms, a microscopic fungus is blocking off the sap conduits, the black insect is exuding its venom.

Dutch Elm Disease, a death sentence on the bark.

On the tapering islets of sand, oleander bushes, isolated, not very tall, scaled down images of the verdant south slope.

Rows of pines on the sloping ledges, long stretches of grass, a pasture up there perhaps, no farm or cabin, no smoke in view.

The solitary climber convinces himself that he's going in the right direction now, should be reassured by that, caught between contentment and indifference still, every event since his departure experienced without emotion or a marked reaction, had he only left to put his mind at rest?

On the off chance, in order to exhaust his luck, to see the truth of so much hearsay with his own eyes?

Or were his senses numbed now as a consequence of that thankless work back there, his unremitting labor in the darkness?

The bitter struggle would've left a dull landscape in its wake, empty of tears and of rage, this journey to the margins would live off that calm, he deserved this calm after so much suffering, so many stifled cries.

His feelings became confused with the effort, interpreting it, concentrating simultaneously on his stride, the swinging of his arms, his respiratory rhythm, working their way into his cadence and bouts of breathlessness, the control of his pace, upsetting his unconscious movement, on this path that never ends.

Feelings on the brink of language, breaking through just before the words, composing the environment surrounding the walker, its immediate appearance or the extreme limit of the sphere drawn by the first radius of his itinerant being, without prejudice toward the infinity around him, crisscrossed with currents and invisible traces tinting his feelings or causing them to fade, depending on the day.

One nascent word worth its weight in enthusiasm, another its easing of tension, the walking speeds up or slows down depending on these unvoiced transmissions, murmured atonally at an un-locatable distance, inaudible to others, negligible within the unearthly range of sounds.

Words passing over the line one single time, leaving the record blank with their passage.

Wert pauses a moment on the path that winds like a mule trail here and there; curving along the gorge, he can make out the sounds of the torrent below, the turbulent waters here spared the slimy reticulations of limestone sediment.

Can no longer see the sea, can see only a fringe of shore, he doubts there's a route over the headland to the east, no one would venture to live in that region.

A hovel with a thatched roof on the opposite hillside, shutters open, the dog has seen the man on the path, charges down as close as he can to the abyss, barks till he's breathless, nobody comes to the door, no fire, no light.

Gray sky, uniform, some clouds up there on the summits, premature tiredness surprises the walker, he's neither hungry nor thirsty however, won't touch his provisions, not before this evening.

A path along a ledge with overhanging rocks, a long, dark, and flat corridor, obstructed with scree, water seeping from the walls, the slabs, it wouldn't be good to stay here, or to sleep.

Wert quickens his step, his lethargy from not too long ago comes back unexpectedly, he doesn't feel it coming, doesn't see himself flag and stagger, losing his composure, collapsing in this tunnel paralyzed with humidity, the night pouring in, a fatal breeze for a fool caught unawares.

Has felt an inopportune drowsiness since leaving his people, since moving away from what he was used to, a drowsiness that washed over him in short, misty waves, this landscape already a long way from that place of training and ordeal, that warlike country so hungry for adventure, he distinguished himself there in his time.

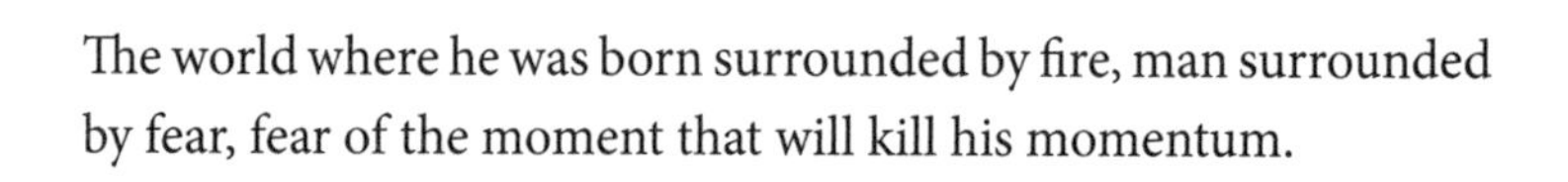

The world where he was born surrounded by fire, man surrounded by fear, fear of the moment that will kill his momentum.

Concealed terror throws him into a panic, packed down tightly under his step, then reappears pale, inassimilable.

Or the terror has transcended tragedy, a flight of the soul, sanctified suffering, malignant fever, all the past to be revisited.

To carve it up in neurotic flashes.

The fear and the dark passageway are gone now, the obstacle of the gorges overcome, the path goes back down a bit, transforms into a series of hollows and rises on a grassy plateau punctuated with holes full of water, the pass between the sister peaks on the horizon of the ridges is its obvious destination.

The high mountain chain and its symmetrical peaks with their snow-covered summits must mark out the eastern boundaries of Wert's known world, the pass must mark the opening toward the next world to the extreme east.

Difficult to make progress without keeping his eye fixed on that gap, looking away from it robs the traveler of his orientation, causes him to wander through the yellowish moss between the puddles for several moments without knowing where he's headed.

Once he locates the reference point again objects resume their places once more as does the object of his quest, that man over there who has forced the boundaries of life, or that's what he was told about him at least, taught at school.

The old man is perhaps nothing more than an antisocial centenarian.

That's all that he knows, all that he left in search of, all that he took off after without putting any more thought into this undertaking that he's still unable to find a proper name for.

Pilgrimage unfitting, adventure too weak.

All the images of the old man that he forms in his mind, sage or not, model themselves unremittingly on classical representations, acquired from books in two ways, through words and images.

Seated under an oak or olive tree, eyes raised, slightly mocking, a forced expression, or just an idiosyncrasy of the model.

The sky remained the same as it appeared in the morning for the entire length of the day, a screen of varied layers of gray, some golden patches lighting it up at times, fleeting circles of light as though cast up from the ground by some distant terrestrial machine.

At other times there's also the particular noise of an aircraft flying faster than the speed of sound, a clear noise, regular, the speed strips away every parameter of one's ability to listen.

The path has become narrow, going upward again toward the pass, searching its way between tufts of mugwort and bushes of euphorbia like strangers on this northern slope.

Then there are only truncated sections of path, to be guessed at right and left thanks to the whims of his stride, which by force of memory seems to find them all by itself.

Wert thinks of taking a break, a bivouac if he dare say it, recalling their camps in the forest of the demon, the places they rested, still on the alert in that country of sweltering heat and of ambush, of guerrilla warfare.

Wild, a deadened shadow fleeing on the earth down below.

And the survivor of those epic feats walks without thinking that he's walking or that he's already walked too much, when he thinks of it he feels the worry weighing him down, hidden up to that point by a clever trick of his conscience.

Tiredness grinds down his spine in this moment at the end of the day, prompting him to jettison his bag, to place it under a walnut tree that he spotted from far off.

The distance at which the pass still appears is not likely to overcome the energy he expects to feel when starting off again in the morning.

A mere hour is all that's needed for the view to radically alter.

The shafts of light on the sea brush the rocky sections of the symmetrical peaks with their dark glints, the nebulous strata, which haven't stopped blocking the sky all day long, diminishing their brightness.

The tree is native to this country, the legends or stories of caravans carrying silks, spices, and strange writings to the far west tell of it.

They say its shadow is harmful, reputedly lethal, they say inexperienced or reckless travelers sleeping in it would never live to wake.

Wert makes a bed of his fears, stretches out at the foot of the tree where, with night falling, soon there's not a living shadow to be seen.

A dream here doesn't include a prelude, actions are already begun, no perceptible connections, colorless outlines, rapid forms before closed eyes, featureless faces, a landscape riddled with blanks.

Unchecked flow in the changing of sets, unstable shiftings that don't allow the eye a hold.

Words torn to pieces, sudden backward surge of sound, it gets extraordinarily loud.

Muttering, short-circuited, breaks up his sleep.

Hallucinated apparition of leaves, stars, the wind like a whip, and the shade of a garden with a path lined with yew trees and a great many stones piled up and scattered across.

A gate, the well and the apple tree, pebbles thrown to the left, to the right, hard as they could.

Murmurings again, murmurings and shouts, the scene becomes strained, body pierced beneath the light.

Someone did something to his stomach.

The griffon uses its paws, tries its best, a chore, dark-purple darkness on the sliced wound, blue-black, saturating the image.

The dream falls apart when he starts awake, doesn't continue, and the wakened traveler besieged by empty terrors doesn't delay in gathering up his things, which have been scattered by the wind, and in eating a frugal meal, lacking fruit and water.

Pale light, the cold of dawn at this altitude, dry cold, it no longer rains since the fisherman set him on the right path.

The clouds have moved off, they're flying south, the gusts of wind mobilize the branches of the big tree, awakening it too, and dead leaves fall to the ground, are already falling in this country, crumpling and creasing.

The mass of leaves covering the space where he'd slept hadn't inhibited his sensations in any respect, or paralyzed his ability, as soon as he was sitting up, to perceive and analyze the situation.

They protected me, put me at ease, he said to himself, they covered my body.

They selected the place where I should sleep on this shapeless hillside.

He takes a few steps with his bag on his back, turns around, contemplates the walnut tree once more, how many of these great trees had he seen in the mountains during combat, looked at without seeing them!

The two peaks are close now, only the snow at the summit makes them seem similar, the one on the left is a little lower, more packed down into itself, its walls, less abrupt, marked with long purple patches.

The one on the right would be called a needle in the western massifs, his childhood summers punctuated with such dizzying escarpments.

With the path pieced together once more, Wert carries on over a floor of slippery, glistening slabs, proper steps in places, while elsewhere scree made up of loose stones cuts across the track, and not many plants to be seen, not many flowers.

Short-stemmed white flowers, their beds level with the ground.

The wind has broken up the cloud formation, he can make out the dark, deep position of the sea, no boats but some slipstreams, maybe the fisherman and his shells are still down there on the shingles, the man who directed him onto the path toward the peaks, does the man scraping the sides of his boat in the dawn make him out now against the light, climbing the slopes on such a fine morning?

The pass would widen as he approached, would open out, and there'd be the tension of discovery, his avid gaze watching for the light to spread, for the dazzling expanse of the open sea.

Primitive land to the east, beyond the limit of the known world, the Ancients pointed it out with their nails as they bent over their rudimentary, mysterious representations, studying them, tablets in hand, tracing lines presumed to exist—in the absence of facts—because symmetrical with those that were already familiar.

The idea that one would be unable to return from there was established early on.

Unpleasant to think that there will be a return even if that return goes without saying, blunts the sharpness of the retreat.

Violent wind coming at him from the side on the final ledge of the ascent, a blast of sea air, it rekindles the faith of the traveler, his purpose.

A few more steps and then a jumble of stones that have been dislodged from the slopes by thaws and runoffs, piled up on the saddle at the juncture of the peaks.

The extreme clarity of the morning coats the peaks and reflects right into his eye, Wert, blinded, pauses, turns around.

A chasm stretches out to the west, an immense reserve of shadow.

Sudden assaults crossing the passes, he'd like to devote all his time to seeing the day, but the clattering of weapons diverts him from it, resounds in his ear, the determination of the guardians of the pass and the blood on the ground, rock, skin.

Blood showing through on the surface, beading, cracking the skin.

End of the first stage, how many more stages, his legs are counting the stones, counting the hours.

To his surprise, the gap between the peaks becomes deeper than expected with every step, a dark trench between the high, sheer walls.

Finds a semblance of a path in places, advances slowly as far as the threshold of the long, elevated passage.

Nothing has hindered his steady progress between the blocks of rock, rivulets flowing around them, dampening his heavy walking shoes, the entry to the new world is open, he approaches it without mishap.

In peacetime, the warrior reflexes lose their edge, all defenses lowered.

Just at the point where he'll start into crossing through the gorge, the long-distance traveler kneels down in front of a narrow pool hollowed out between two rocks, hands cupped, drinks the ice-cold water.

Moves the rocks apart a little, plunges his flask into the pool.

The water bubbles into the bottleneck, fills the gourd with little spurts, overflowings, and Wert feels his ankle paralyzed, anaesthetized in an instant, as though cut from his body.

Alien, ripped from his body.

The pain came, he sees the creature with its black segments slipping between the rocks, sting pointed skyward.

Saw only the sting, removed in one go, the sting named the creature and he saw the pincers, the black segments.

And the curved appendage.

Sat down on the stones, his ankle is swelling, a dark purple web makes a pattern on his skin.

Caught unawares, his perception has divided in two, projected into two scenes, the real scene of his journey, and the narrated scene of this journey, as written, published, illustrated with vignettes.

You see him close to a pool in the sketch, rolling up the left leg of his trousers, examining the wound.

Further on, he's trying to bind his leg with a strap from his bag, gets tangled up, makes many attempts.

A photo frames him leaning against a rock, feeling his ankle, his foot.

At times, the figures on the two pictures coincide, and here he is distraught, gesticulating, grimacing.

Something is wrong in his link to the place, a hesitation in his movements betrays the discrepancy, you force him to stick to the scene, he rebels.

Gives up, lets go.

Virtual place, virtual body, one or the other, not both.

Wert, dazed, looks in front of him, prostrate, he tries to go back to the time of the sting, to reverse it.

Doesn't dare look at his leg, casts another glance over the flesh, which is going black, blistering here, cracking there, continuing to swell, the flesh on his calf, his knee.

Instinctively, he looks for shelter from the wind, moves as he can along the rock, leans on his right elbow and heel, heaves, the sick leg follows.

The bag impedes this maneuver, so heavy, he pulls the straps toward him after every crawl, the bag gets caught on stones, hits the leg.

This means of crawling brings him little by little into the well-sheltered area at the foot of the rock, he sits with his back against the still-damp rock face.

Catches his breath, would collect his wits too if only they'd go along with the relentless course of events, what to do to stabilize the scene, so that time and space would coexist again in his sight?

So that they'd readjust, converge again in the thick of this moment, all actions plausible, the words in his head too?

The sun already high in the sky, blinding, the blood in his leg feels heavier, throbs haltingly, is it the blood, the poison that's blackening his leg, blood and venom mixing together, another body inside his own.

The tourniquet doesn't hold, the muscle gradually turns a dark color, overripe stains under the knee become integrated with the main current, he grips his knee between his clammy hands, forces his leg to bend.

The area surrounding the wound is no longer recognizable within the massive swelling, except an infinitesimal point close to the heel, is that the point of the sting?

The curved tail of the monster is constantly etched before the eyes of the wounded, that last inverse segment of the stinger, the fleeing animal brandishing the threat again, sting pointed back toward its victim.

That strange structure is familiar to him, it used to intrigue him in the desert, some of the men used to trap the animal in a circle of flames, waiting in vain for its myth to die along with it.

Nothing in his bag to counteract the venom, Wert is losing hope, can do nothing but follow the progress of the vile substance polluting his veins.

And the water, the water from the flask spilled during the unpredictability of the drama.

The wall is seeping within his reach, his fingers become soaked in ice-cold water, he coats his mouth, his eyes with it.

The agony of contraction and inflexibility of his limbs, a surge of intense pain, moving around only serves to exacerbate the ascent of the injected liquid from the miniscule sting.

Crying out or moaning only speeds the flow.

And the scenes separate once more, did he ever climb up here, must have stayed close to the fisherman, it's not he who's dying.

Wild, a phantom in the thick, silent, amnesiac cloud.

Gusts of wind beating against his back, blowing from the west, the west is driving him away while, in front of him, the world of promises is closing up.

Can make out nothing aside from the long corridor between the steep slopes of the gorge, the backlighting eliminates the pale surfaces, only the dark and streaming walls show through.

Postpones the moment of looking closely at the progress of the poison, undoes his pants, the slow tide pervades every pore of his skin, inundates the villi, has reached his thigh and lower abdomen.

Dark purple, and those white points, inner flocculation, a yellow streak at the groin.

A reticulation that nothing can stop and his heart pounds, clattering in his head, ears, and throat, a wild beating that weakens the memory, connection to life.

Fever, terror of a dehiscence of his organs, of his skin fraying, what's creeping through his blood vessels is tainting his mind, distorting it, debasing the words.

He who's being altered by the mingled blood and venom must have lost consciousness at some point during the height of the sun's radiance, midday perhaps, his weakened eyes couldn't withstand the glare.

Dizzy spell, light-headedness, a negativity takes root.

More than somnolence, a collapse warped by the pain and the madness of resisting it, under the pressure of fever a certain force had chosen to cede and release its hold, he's been carrying that force within, wasn't aware of it, since when has he carried it?

He is here in the blackness, no longer feels his body or else no longer has a body, except for his eye, which sees little, his ear, which hears little.

Where he is, there is nothing to hear or see for the moment, every moment, a lifelessness, a lethargy cradles him, it's an understatement to say he's not thinking of anything, doesn't dream, doesn't imagine anything tangible.

The force in him has renounced pride, his body is becoming a thing like every thing that surrounds him, and lymph, plasma, like water and sap.

His blood will bead, will ooze out, will drain away outside him, or rise even further in his artery, will taint, corrupt his heart.

Will taint his knowledge, his loved ones, his inculcated ideas, those he believed were his and signed in his blood.

Lines very soon broken, indecisive forms, images taking a long time to light up on a pale screen, no color, sound doesn't penetrate, a dream fails to take shape at the heart of his torpor, doubly impoverished and melancholy from sleeping.

The stupor disarms his senses, his apathy negates the extreme pain, what threshold had he crossed there, the question wavers on the screen of the non-dream, gets lost beyond substance.

State of stupor, his life working at the threshold of non-life, a shock sets aside this light-headedness, the night comes, and the cold.

In the half-light, Wert sees the line of puffiness under his skin, from ankle to knee, already spreading over his thigh.

A duct bent at an angle, lumpy, conquered, running over stiff flesh, chewed, swallowed, twisted.

A short abandoned variant: the creature touched the bone.

Goes around at its leisure, observes the patient, journeys into his body, I feel every pinch, every bite, all this negligible, I was suffering more under the sun.

The beast goes astray as I often do, turns back, finds the right path, knows where it's going, certainly, certainly better than I do.

The one I'm heading toward in that country isn't expecting me, do I even know where he lives, I know his name, renowned as immortal, is it his real name that the country's Ancients revealed to me?

I didn't write it down, what need have I for the letters themselves?

Contorted grimace, the animal strikes a nerve, twists it, and the lifeless figure observes with curiosity what becomes of the body when its constituents crack, and its integrity.

Torpor gains the upper hand, exhaustion carries him off, a sudden numbness cuts into his fingers.

The world has taken its nocturnal form, the wind from the west has dropped, the moon in its first quarter casts a glimmer of light over the neighboring rocks that guide his eyes.

Anaesthetized, Wert experiences this semi-dulling of pain in the absence of reference points, he has lost his bearings in the night, their distinctive features.

Knows that whatever is watching over and working within him is a diabolical being, unlikely, spiked.

Vicious, it tears the skin with its pedipalps, the black blood spurts and spills on the surrounding stones.

The creature has broken through his navel, frees itself of the visceral magma bit by bit, relentless machine foraging and gnawing, scratching, enlarging the exit of its tunnel.

It only knows how to lick the blood, to suck it, to gulp it, the blood pours out, extravasates, his lower abdomen and genitals soaked in heavy, sticky liquid.

The paralyzed traveler observes with interest how the ringed body of the scorpion drags itself from his own, leaves behind it the sinuous swelling of the egress that took so long to excavate.

Places his hand between his lower abdomen and the creature in a token effort, pathetic, his fingers narrowly miss the pincers, what would another sting matter after this meticulous devastation?

The outlandish animal comes to a standstill a moment, moves away, a red thread hangs from its jaws.

Without doubt the worn-out hiker imagined that the enemy would give up, would abandon this human body and its hideous interior, would slide back under a rock.

Alarmed, he closed his eyes.

Goes back to the scene of blackness, focused on the screen where figures are finally beginning to take shape.

The torturer's itinerary differed somewhat from that fantasized about by its victim, the black creature is projected upon the background of the gorge, between the peaks, enlarged out of all proportion on this white canvas.

The thing confronting Wert is a living being that seems to see him, to stare at him, even, hieratic, barring the entry to the gorge in the background.

Waiting for the other to do something, say something, it would be up to him to demonstrate.

I am not welcome, it seems.

No one has penetrated this gorge yet, nobody has ever taken such a path!

I will cross that gorge in spite of the obstacles, I will get to the end of my path.

If that's the way it must be, the pass is clear, may you reach the end of your journey safe and sound!

The image of the zealous guardian of the pass begins to fade, is fading quickly, the whole scene disappears in no time and Wert finds himself alone once more at the foot of his rock.

He sees the glow of dawn appearing through the gorge, the biting cold grabs him.

Stiff, exhausted, he examines ankle and leg, groin and knee, a dark streak fringed with violet blotches marks the furrow drilled beneath the skin by the scorpion during its frightening intrusion into his body.

Sees that at the center of his abdomen, the lips of the unbearable fissure are beginning to heal together.

Notices with relief the general delitescence of the swelling and of the inflammatory symptoms that had lasted the whole night.

Crawls as far as the pool, washes off the blood that's clotted the length of his leg as far as his hip, scrapes the scabs from his lower-abdomen, wipes off the film of sticky, amber-colored liquid that leaked down between his thighs.

Scrubs insistently, removes the many bits of dead flesh stuck to his skin one by one.

Cleans his pants as best he can, tidies himself, puts shirt and jacket back in order.

Retrieves his flask, goes to fill it from a pool further upstream, larger, far from the one that caused the disaster.

Drinks several mouthfuls of ice-cold water, isn't terribly thirsty, strangely enough, has to start walking again, to reeducate his leg, find once more the strolling rhythm of his body, a balance, the right tempo.

His mind feels clear, as clear as it can be after such a night, his head relieved of its weight.

This unexpected display, the composure in his voice must have defeated the guardian of this place.

That warrior creature on the screen, black bands tightly linked, pincers wide open, sting standing up after piercing him, what other weapon against it than words?

With a pronounced slight limp for the first steps, Wert with his bag on his back feels weighed down with this violence added to the pain, expends an enormous amount of energy, feeling for his footing at each step forward with a hesitant and timid leg.

Bent forward determinedly, doesn't even turn around, not a glance to the west where the dark end of the night still conceals everything.

Only fears slipping on the stones where the water is frozen in patches.

Starts into the rocky passage that the eastern light is carving up, raises his eyes toward the two peaks on either side of his route, can only make out their outlines and the banks of snow up high.

Moves forward cautiously, watchful of the terrain, barely looks around him, or does so almost unconsciously, brought back to the hallucinatory nocturnal combat.

Realizes suddenly that he's reached the exit.

A few more steps and the frightful walls fall away, release their hold, the glimmers of daybreak light up the pass at his back, make it seem far less arduous and disturbing than it had appeared from the other side.

Without a doubt he'd walked more than he thought, must have readjusted faster than he'd hoped, his strength quickly recovered, his leg no longer pitching him forward at every molehill.

The country he's entered on the other side intrigues him, he gets only fragmentary, dislocated impressions of it, intermittent glimmers of light pass over it.

The backlighting filters out the pale surfaces, only the dark areas show through, a forest perhaps, an old lava flow, the vast course of a river cloaked in mist.

Who had spoken of a desert, and of crossing it in order to join he whose secret fuels the traveler's fever, keeps him moving onward?

Immortality, intransitive of terror, a sheath of ice freezes your sword.

He could have forfeited his life at the entrance to the gorge between the pincers of that insidious demon with its arched, venomous tail.

Had he really thought he was going to die up there, a decaying carcass stuck to his rock, rotten flesh, decomposing fingers, the worms coming out of his nostrils?

Would never have seen his homeland again, never seen his people.

But this new country quickly diverts him from his past, which knew neither tranquility nor gentleness.

The shimmerings had multiplied.

The further he advanced into this land that glistened with ice, the more those layers of ice, flattened over every rock or branch in the great morning cold, would twinkle.

He found himself quickly surrounded by gems that glittered and seemed to converge toward him, glints of intersecting lights, bunches of fruit enchanting the eye.

Could no longer find the path.

This lasted the length of time it took to descend part way.

A few moments later, when the rising sun's rays were hitting objects from a different angle, the walker himself now changing his perspective, the way his gaze cut through the light, the spell vanished in an instant.

No obsidian or agate, turquoise or cornelian, instead he found himself in a high mountain pasture, the alpine flowers and plants forming a blanket from a distance, they parted at his approach and were scattered about in pale-colored tufts.

Further down there were trees, pines, cedars perhaps, blackberry bushes often forced him to turn around, he'd retrace his steps.

And always the river in the distance.

He stumbled upon a path that certainly seemed to lead down from the pass, and that he hadn't noticed in the phantasmagoria of daybreak, or else it was coming from elsewhere, from another gorge, the shepherds would take it when moving their livestock to other pastures at the turn of the seasons.

Further down, there were carob trees, vines, it was starting to get hot, the newcomer to this agreeable country can later make out a faint dirt track down below, ruts marked by tire tracks.

He went as far as this track, sat on a rock, following the tracks with his eyes to the right, the left, wondering from which direction the vehicle that possibly crossed and re-crossed here every morning would come and give him a lift.

He would hear the noise, would locate its origin quickly, would see the vehicle through the thick bushes before it came into view completely.

The atmosphere was heating up as morning progressed in the valley that seemed to have formed in this spot as a result of the convergence of several surrounding ravines.

It was a calm, pleasant place; if he had to remain a long time waiting, he would withdraw to the cover of the light foliage close by.

For the moment, he was catching his breath, had come down too quickly perhaps, putting his ravaged leg and frayed joints—filed down by the barbaric progress of the tenacious sentinel's venom—too much to the test.

He got up again, did a few limbering exercises, satisfied himself that every part of his battered carcass was reacting correctly to his brain's solicitations.

There was still a certain reluctance in his ankle and the persistent sense of a tightness in the groin, all scrapes obliterated but still hurting him just as much as before.

He moved his bag to the shade of a pistachio tree, neither cedars nor walnuts on the southern mountainside, lay down on the dead leaves.

Satisfied at having convinced the small creature to grant him passage in the end, he already has trouble believing that even dying would have released him from his old moth-eaten yoke, had he been left for dead between two patches of frozen water.

In a short while, he'd no longer think back over this episode, any more than he still did a number of other, similar ones, childhood stories from the old days, he had crossed the pass like one of those trainee heroes on the path to fairy-tale fame, that's all there was to it.

The heat was rising, a certain torpor permeated the landscape, he took off his thick leather jacket and folded it to use as a pillow, then lay on his back facing the sky, where strange, white knots way up high seemed for the moment completely motionless.

The air was only disturbed by gentle breezes in the branches of the small tree, and an intermittent tinkling, that of fresh water splashing between the rocks at some distance from the road.

He was thirsty and needed to get up, stayed down, saw that every cloud had evaporated.

Closed his eyes, head as empty as the sky.

Are you going to take a nap or hop in?

The man at the steering wheel was leaning out of the cabin toward him, he called out in a strong voice that didn't exactly rise above the noise of the engine.

Wert got up with a start, had assembled his belongings in no time at all and circled the 4x4, jumped nimbly on board.

Was barely awake, slowly getting his thoughts together amid the jolts of a road that was badly maintained, if at all, casting glances at the driver to his left who was squeezed into a gray-green jacket covered in red dust, a forest warden maybe; the Astrakhan hat thrust down as far as his eyebrows gave him the appearance of a bandit.

Bent over the steering wheel, drove without worrying about the ruts, shovels and pickaxes bouncing around in a clear, uninterrupted din.

The route followed the valley without too many detours, there were meadows bordering it now, it was also possible to make out, a long way back, the ridgeline and the pass that cut through it, very narrow between its glistening walls of ice.

You've come from up there?

Affirmative sign from the passenger, the driver starts to laugh, you must've had trouble up there, everyone says they had a lot of trouble up there.

All of those picked up on the road where the path ends up, in fact.

It's true, the route is very hazardous; I've come from the west, far over there to the west.

There are wars over there, many wars, that's what they say around here.

The river interrupted the track, the man slowed down, drove through in first gear, the vehicle rattled for a while over the pebbles, some water went over the hood, squirted onto the windscreen.

On the other bank, a completely different landscape unfurled, terraced cultivations, steep slopes on the hillsides, a village far below.

Almond trees on the terraces and rectangles of barley, some patches of broad beans under an irrigation channel, tomatoes, more vineyards and reams of hops, the road descended in twists, met the spate again further down, became less steep as far as the cob houses.

Walls of yellowish-brown earth and straw, flat roofs covered in maize drying under the full heat of the sun, some children suddenly appeared, ran after the car, shouted as they do everywhere in the world.

There were other villages and other children's shouts, the driver drove carefully now, without any sudden stops, barely touching the steering wheel, as though assured that, everything being in order now that they'd arrived on the plain, he could let his engine run by itself and even close his eyes.

A perceptible harmony emanated from this country, Wert enjoyed it without feeling surprise, he'd known for a long time now—perhaps from some vision passing rapidly before his eyes—that he would one day drive through a peaceful country like this one.

Fields of cotton to the right, to the left fields of poppies with a peppery smell that stung the nostrils, the now asphalt road was approaching the river.

I'll leave you here, said the man in the green, dust-covered clothes, you see the market town over there, there's a garrison, a canteen, they'll find you a bed for the night.

He stopped in front of a garden full of enormous squashes and pumpkins, the traveler jumped to the ground, took up his bag, his jacket.

The driver then turned toward him, spoke to him frankly, in a voice without intonation now, monotonous, impersonal.

You've come to see Xian—you too?

Wert at that moment can no longer recognize the driver's features, his slightly mocking eyes have become cold, a coldness without animosity, simply distant, and with an intense brightness, memorable.

The 4x4 takes off almost without a sound and the passenger is left alone, dazed on the roadway, sees the vehicle move off slowly, disappear after a short distance behind a row of cypress trees.

Finds himself thus alone on the road that's straight as far as the first houses of the market town, vans pass him by, carts carrying poultry and sacks of grain, peasants pushing sheep and goats ahead of them.

Can still make out the line of the mountains on the horizon, so far away now, lost in the haze at some considerable distance, he must have certainly dozed off, slept a long time, they'd driven a lot farther than he thought.

The sun at its zenith covers the bank of the river with a heavy dampness, the newcomer to this patch of earth mops the sweat from his forehead, moves forward with difficulty, legs heavy, short of breath every ten paces.

Groups rushing along at a fast clip, still not very talkative, passing him without staring at him, even his big leather jacket doesn't attract attention.

He walks without turning around anymore, sleepy, unappreciative of the surroundings, sleepwalking in broad day.

Finds himself walking, after a time, along a street lined with shops and stalls with their wares spread out right on the ground, didn't notice at what point he entered the town.

Down a perpendicular lane he notices a sailboat, an expanse of water with barely a ripple, the end of a quay.

At that moment, a foghorn rings out, from a steamboat casting off or returning to port, and all the noises that he was barely hearing up to now rush in on him in a single burst, flooding his ears in an instant.

Eardrums assailed with cries, shouting, intricate exchanges in the throng, with a growing intensity, a lot louder than he's accustomed to.

Then, he hears the language of this place, the one all these people around him are speaking.

Tells himself at first that he doesn't understand, the unexpected emphases accentuate it, the strong consonants dilute the adjoining sounds, subordinate them to their formation, to their system, their law.

On another level, however, he can understand this language, the words aren't continuously unintelligible to him, he catches their form at times, guesses their meaning, as if his ear was adapting in fits and starts, was fleetingly changing its method of listening, tuned to a simultaneous translation, not very exact, or precise, but sufficient nevertheless to retain what was essential.

They're talking about a big flood, the storm hit the coast to the north, devastated roads and villages, drowned livestock and fields, a sole family survived, when the water level fell their boat was perched on a rock.

About a feast day next month as well, in honor of a holy man or a foreign prince, there Wert gets out of his depth, preparations, celebrations, everything becomes confused.

The strange thing is that he's not really surprised at the phenomenon, after a few moments he simply enjoys it, without asking himself questions, takes visible pleasure in it, this will make things easier, he thinks, is cheered by it.

Continued to follow the town's main artery at a slow pace, considering the stalls with curiosity, and with longing a tiny shop where fruits unknown to him were displayed on a bed of dead leaves, bluish bananas, red grapes with long twisted bunches, others whose names he doesn't know, greenish balls with ringed sides, as though chiseled by a man's hand.

He points at one of the appetizing spheres, proffers a note from his distant country, without batting an eyelid the shopkeeper hands him back a fistful of coppers with a golden glint, imprinted with a dove.

Change from this new place, its glint illuminating the dark room with its singular fragrances.

Few tall houses in the small town, no public building in view, is that a church, a temple, a mosque over there, that building next to a cylindrical bell tower of pale stone?

Wert notices a wooden bench in a square planted with araucarias that are flattened toward the west by the dominant wind, relieves himself of his load, settles himself down comfortably, eats his way through the ripe fruit.

More bitter than anticipated, and the sweetness comes afterward, fresh and sweet, fulfills him.

A foreigner here savoring the peculiar fruit, curious about the language, listening.

Two girls sitting behind him confide flings and flames to one another, their voices enchant him, whispered birdsong.

Raising his eyes, he notices on the other side of the street a flag with a short pole whose colors take a while to unfurl, the fabric hangs, folds lying still in the sweltering heat.

In front of the doorway into the small, redbrick construction, not of great scale, a soldier stands guard, weapon at his foot.

Rested, Wert gets up, starts walking again, jacket in one hand, bag in the other, heads off with measured steps in the direction of the barracks, the people are already leaving again in little groups, carts rattling over the paved street.

The soldier doesn't look the least bit special, resting his back against a pillar of the door, seems absent, despite everything the word canteen sounds familiar to his ear, his hand points out a long sloping roof adjacent to the barracks, set back from the road just before the osier bed.

At a corner of the barracks the traveler is seized by an image, a log hut at the corner of a castle, abandoned, demolished by an ancient storm.

The forest protects it, surrounds it.

Wert knocks on the glass window of the door, the curtain is pulled back, a gray eye behind the windowpane, motionless, doesn't settle directly on him, its face sheathed with a hazy film, inexpressive.

The curtain falls back, the door doesn't open, Wert waits a bit, knocks again, the bolt is slid back, the door opens a crack.

The eyes seem to stare through without seeing him, the face belongs to quite a young woman with a very pale complexion, a red headscarf tied at the nape of her neck encircles black hair, her blouse with its very loose-fitting folds ensures great freedom of movement.

She's bargaining with her fear, the intruder thinks, she's weighing the risks.

I saw you arriving from a long way off, who are you, you're a drifter, where are you headed for along this shore?

Wert sees some tables inside the room, the room is empty, no noise coming from it, or from the kitchens either.

Where is everyone, nobody's here today?

Be on your way, I can tell you're bad luck.

You don't know me, and I know I don't have a pleasant appearance, but what reason do you have to distrust me, it was the forester who sent me.

After another wait, during which opposing arguments battled in her head, difficult to decide, the canteen lady gradually opened the door, still showing signs of reluctance.

Wert enters the low-ceilinged room, larger than he'd expected, fifty odd tables are lined up in strict order, a counter gleams at the back, and some bottles, pots, then vats further back, and a trestle table holding earthenware jars.

The woman has closed the door again, slid the bolt back, they're out on an exercise today, she says.

She stands in front of him, scrutinizes him for a long time, intensely, an intense stare can reveal everything about a person in no time at all, honors, escapades, and dangers, likewise acts of cruelty, weaknesses.

Adventures.

The forester led you to me, you waited for him on the path from the pass, you crossed the gap between the Twins, you conquered the guardian of the pass.

She speaks with her eyes lowered, going over the story again to fix it in her memory.

They sat down at a table, she went as far as the counter, filled two large glasses, they drink the beer in little sips, some carts still pass from time to time on the way from the osier bed back to the fields beyond, fields of peppers, hops, and then the rice fields to the north.

Wert is relaxed at last, here before this woman in whom he can no longer sense suspicion, she's on my side, he thinks, that of the marauders, of the migrants in a country with a nomad past.

This place and the surrounding area accept him—flat, lush country after so much rockiness, perceptible nearness of the river, he was thirsty, very thirsty on coming in here.

You climbed the slopes of the pass, walked along the ominous shore, a fisherman spoke to you, before that I don't know.

Wert feels himself taken backward, two stories collide within him, the mountain and its pass have altered the tenses of narration, changed their flow, the points of emphasis, have silently worked on his words.

He remains there searching for the words and their destinations in a sentence, pompous speech has no place on this side of the mountain, he searches for simple words, unadorned words, but it's the same words as ever that elect themselves, do what he might, he can't escape them.

It was I who conquered the Guardian of the Forest of the Cedars, it was I who killed the Winged Bull, it was I . . .

His voice gives out after this bold beginning, he forced it too much, or else the famous story has suddenly escaped him.

Wild, fleeting shadow silently listening under the earth below.

Was the woman really listening, she doesn't react, his words in their vehement flow demanded a continuation, but her guest remains silent, his eyes lost, far from his town and from his glory.

A little later, she'll say: if it was you who did those things, why are you here looking so poor, so destitute, so alone?

Wert seems constrained in his words, numbed, he'd like to respond to the canteen lady, will form a response but the words will come apart in his throat, will barely pass his lips, or else his words just don't have the same form, the same force in this country.

The same meaning.

The long journey has restructured his sensations, reworked his images, how they're framed, their vividness, the horrors becoming more varied, his dreadful, haunting grief diluted.

An endless moment of silence now reigns in the room, audible, every inch of ground, every corner as though soundproofed, quilted, spaces designed with such care, such subtlety, implying a new order.

The woman observes him carrying out this delicate transfer in the weighing of signs, grouping his emotions according to new affinities.

Certainly he is having difficulty in transposing a memory from the former world into a memory from this present one, placing it in another part of his mind, especially if it's a question of his memory of a painful event.

The intervening time he's lived through makes it difficult to access manageable snippets of memory, he finds himself trying to put them together again according to new laws, he can only grab them and repeat them to himself off the cuff, beaten into a vague order, barely comprehensible, definitely unreliable.

His body against mine, my friend, seven days I mourned him, his eyes fading, seven nights, his forehead turning blue, the flesh of his stomach, his hands, the poison spreading without slowing, he can no longer speak, no longer moan.

This decay cast on the earth, I don't want to see the horror of the body, this icy weight on my heart, my fingers clay dust, my eyelids, my eyes.

I fled the horror of my friend's body, fled its features showing through in my own mortal body, worms sprang up in him before my eyes, bored through his flesh, what I saw still taunts me, observes me.

Intransitive of terror, nonexistent immortality.

The daylight in the fragile building made of planks is quickly fading now, the visitor will confide no more, has said all he could say, told about his journey up to this point.

The woman respects his silence, what happens next doesn't belong to her, she will do her best to facilitate its beginnings.

He could make out the very pale oval of her face, the red patch of the head scarf circling her hair against her temples.

Her gray eyes stared at him as they had at first without giving the impression of fully seeing the soothing of his features, perhaps these moments seemed remote to her, she had seen so many of them in this place of passage.

Wert had been quiet for a long time, felt something like a hiatus in the flow of the story, his own or that of his travels.

A gap in the scene from the canteen.

A fragment must have been lost, interpolated spontaneously, the story altered somewhat.

The tablet chipped.

Xian lives over on the other bank, says the canteen lady, only the boatman knows where to find his retreat, he'll bring you there tomorrow, if the wind picks up.

She delivered these words in one go, as if they went without saying, then lead the visitor into a small shed furnished with a table and a camp bed.

You can sleep here if you want, he'll come and get you tomorrow.

The room looks out over the river, Wert makes out the rocks in the dim light, the glint of the lights on the moving water, says he's happy to finally see the river.

The woman laughs, is surprised.

But that's the sea!

The traveler has the night ahead of him to recall this word in every language, the canteen lady articulated it oddly, prolonged the syllable as though to magnify the feeling of openness, an iodized flavor, the timber streaming with backwash from the waves, the unsettled vastness glimpsed in the sound of the letters.

Vastness doesn't mean eternity of space, breathed a malicious voice in the ear of the sleeper, eternity doesn't spell immortality for the body . . .

He passes a calm night, once he's finally lying down, can relax to his heart's content after the excessive gymnastics of his hiking escapade, he smells salt and algae through the open window.

Finds the big room empty in the morning, canteen lady called by the supply corps into town, she's left some fruit on a table, some bread for her tramp of the day.

He leaves through the concealed door at the back of the building, goes as far as the cliff, notices a sandy creek below, it's there that the one who'll take charge of him will berth.

He descends the slippery crag, some flowers in the hollows of the rocks, daisies, primroses, some types of thistles.

The boatman is ready, sitting at the back of a small craft four or five meters long and anchored close to the beach, may have been waiting a long time in this position, on an assignment in any case, on orders, or so the woman gave Wert to understand.

Cap with a leather peak, a black oilskin falling almost to his feet, stooping figure, watching the horizon, the sea mist that covers it.

The man didn't hear his passenger coming, turns around in a flash, face tanned, copper-colored, small eyes set under thick eyebrows.

Carefully examines the heavily burdened stranger whose fading line of footprints indicate his progress toward the other shore.

Expresses himself with parsimonious, composed phrases, they come through his lips as soon as he needs them, they aren't forced, they don't seem to be prompted by the silent course of any preliminary reflections, his gentle lisp preventing his interlocutor from grasping certain words, or else Wert simply doesn't recognize them.

It's better if it doesn't clear too quickly, he says.

You can see the fog shifting in quick streaks, sliding like panels stacking up and reorganizing themselves, according to what system do they rise, then fall back to the surface of the water?

Overcast sky, calm sea, hardly a ripple, a fringe of kelp peters out noiselessly on the ochered sand.

The man in black seems in no hurry to leave, is waiting for the tide no doubt, it's a matter of a narrow channel, reefs whose position he knows by heart.

His initial posture hasn't changed, still watching the distance, squinting at times to better make out a detail of the view there on the moving cloud front.

All of a sudden he's moving, rushes to the bow of the boat, water up to his waist, lifts the anchor, come and help then, shouldn't delay any longer now, push!

Wert added his efforts to those of the sailor, in no time the sailboat is pulling away, the two of them heave themselves on board.

As there is no wind at the coast, the man resorts to the auxiliary motor, the start-up poses a problem, he tries it over and again.

Finally, the small boat clears the creek and the cliffs on either side begin to lose some of their grandeur, become gradually integrated to the shoreline in an unbroken continuity.

The harbor appears on their right, the old town in the background, not as vast as the traveler thought the day before, he was tired yesterday, didn't have all his wits about him.

Has the impression that since waking things have moved very quickly, will continue at this favorable, providential pace, for the moment the frail skiff is barely moving.

We'll try to find the wind further north, at the edge of the fog, it will protect us from onlookers, the ferryman announces obligingly, as though giving a tour.

One hand firmly holds the tiller, the other gropes the motor where there's constantly something to adjust.

Soon the little sailboat enters the blanket of cloud, you can't see ten feet in front of you, leaning forward, Wert tries to detect the narrow channel where they must change course amid the shifting vapors, the place where the expert knows to head north and find the wind.

He's enjoying this game in which the immense fluctuating surface of the water is concealed then revealed, far from the arid escarpments above and their deathtraps.

To a hidden place, its access-point secret, the mist would be their accomplice; what does he do in fair weather, wonders the novice, doesn't risk it no doubt, the seeker must wait for days on the cliff at the outset, beseeching the squall, the storm.

To circle around the obstacle as one circles around the mystery of a place and of its guardian, though here the fog isn't an obstacle, but a safeguard.

A screen.

To circle around the word when it doesn't want to deliver up its form, to suggest it by its reflections in the water.

Understatement, periphrasis, Wert unintentionally gives himself up to devices that make him feel far from comfortable, rhetoric borrowed from a transitory reflection.

Nevertheless, the breeze makes itself felt, the mainsail swells in fits and starts, droops back down again, stretches out with a dry snap, and the sailboat leans into the waves, picks up speed.

The coast hasn't been visible for some time now, the motor has gone quiet, the swash of the water cracking against the obstacle of the boat seems exceptionally silent after the intrusive roar of the engine.

Settled comfortably, the boatman navigates with ease, satisfied with this slight wind flying them eastward at a good clip, brings his attention back to his passenger, but then, had the sailor's half-open, half-closed eyes behind their supercilious screen left Wert for a single moment?

Why are you so thin, your features so sunken, your body so weak, I imagined you more restless, more warlike, the man in black says finally, as though summing up all the impressions he'd formed since the appearance of the foreigner on the cliff in the morning.

Not receiving a response, he remains silent a moment, watching the sky that the wind has cleared of its cloudy screen, making a slight course correction from time to time.

She told me that you had crossed the pass, that you came from far away, she's a little talkative, it's none of my business of course.

I've come from a long way off, it's true, says Wert simply, I waged war, travelled to my heart's content, now I've left my city, my people, I am walking my path alone.

The Master has heard talk of you, the boatman continues, as though settling in for a real conversation, but a violent blast of wind makes him leap up and take down the sails.

Further blasts of wind then, more violent still, and the pilot rushed around, tacked, adjusted the sail in the moments of calm.

Shortly afterward, the gust of a gale blew in, and the small boat listed, braced itself.

The currents are colliding, it's the maelstrom, the primordial sea, shouted the boatman over the noise, hold on tight! don't let go!

Wert jumped up, went as far as the mast, clasped it with one arm; with the other he put his bag away in the shallow compartment for inanimate objects, provisions, luggage.

He was standing in the center of the boat now, could barely see any farther than from his post in the bow, but this position suited him, the spot where one is least thrown around in a storm.

The swell sprang up and grew larger before his eyes, total chaos, interlaced undulations of every scale and shape, the novelty of this situation captivated him, he'd never imagined the sea in such turmoil, these waters of death, such fury.

The man at the tiller concentrated on his arduous work, his body stiff, taking in the whole horizon with his gaze, anticipating his boat's reactions, knew this particular, difficult place.

At one point, a wave from the side almost overturned the craft; the surprised passenger wasn't really scared, he didn't move, didn't cry out.

Felt himself to be the object of a strange transference, put back in an old position, his child's body standing up very straight on the bridge, contemplating the ocean, the captain at his side aiming his telescope at a none-too-agreeable land.

The surface of the water was completely calm, the boat was sliding along, an ideal demonstration, almost noiselessly, directly along its route.

When this swap comes to an end, Wert abandons himself to the sliding of the sailboat over the flat water, the sun is going down, his back is to the mast, before him the eastern shore is emerging with infinite slowness.

A mild breeze from the northwest now, irregular, imperceptible at times, obliging the boatman to change speed often, altering course slightly each time.

Silvery-gray water, dark blue picking up the red reflections of the sunset, yellow and mauve patches stretched out, tremulous, the traveler kneels down, leans over to wash his hands.

Don't touch that water! shouts the man at the tiller, Wert's movement had pulled him out of his somnolence and seemed to frighten him far more than made sense.

The startled traveler draws back his hand, wipes it automatically on his jacket, his eyes questioning.

That water was deadly at one time, they say that it still carries traces of poison!

Disconcerted by this incident, doubting he'd really escaped harm, Wert went to sit down in the bow, became absorbed in the gradual unfolding of the new continent.

Saw an island rise up with rounded summits, bared in the full light from the dying rays of the sun, a dark patch mid-slope that might have been a forest.

Saw two islands, three islands, the same shape and bright color, not as high as the first, a dense forest rising there as far as the ridge.

Later the flamboyant aspect of the archipelago faded, everything seemed closer, the low parts joined together little by little into a continuous shoreline, the traveler realized that a single and vast land was laid out before him.

You see the estuary between the two hills, that's where my cabin is, tonight you'll sleep at my place.

The sun had disappeared, the wind blew stronger for a moment, calmed at their approach to the coast, the man maneuvered skillfully, a line of reefs stood between the shore and the little sailboat.

In the daylight that was rapidly fading, a lot more rapidly than on the land they'd left behind, Wert catches glimpses of some giant trees leaning over the shore.

Neither eucalyptus nor palm trees, he's unable to name them, the pilot when consulted offers names which sound new to his ear.

With the sail drawn in, the boat anchored very close to the shore, the two men got a foothold on the shingle, advanced in the crepuscular glow that was transformed soon afterward, once they'd passed the first trees, into a shadowy light only pierced by pale gleaming spindles.

It's on the ledge up there overlooking the mouth of the river, said the boatman, it's not far, it's a bit steep.

The narrow path between the low branches and the thorn bushes rose in fits and starts, the newcomer, still dazed from the blasts of the storm, clothes soaked through, struggled to put his foot higher with each step on a forest floor he imagined was made of pine needles and dead leaves.

It was as if he had been sailing for months on a stormy sea, he panted, took rests, saw his guide moving away from him with steady strides, saw him disappear and reappear, fade into the half-light, still he couldn't ask the boatman to carry his bag.

Strangely, the sailor wasn't carrying one, walked on the firm ground in his long black coat, paying attention to the wind, spending his hours imperturbably without ever having a rest, slackening a moment, neither eating nor drinking.

With a narrow facade, as though inserted or wedged between two boulders, the cabin was a construction with a rustic appearance, part log, part bamboo, the thatched roof with its two slopes attested the fact that it must rain a lot in the region.

Turned out to be bigger than expected inside, rudimentary but apposite in the darkness that had rapidly extended to the entire mountainside.

The lord of the manor lit a carbide lamp, prepared a meal, cleared crates, pots, spread out a second mat close to the door.

Exhausted, Wert didn't have much of an appetite, barely touched the rice and dried fish his host offered him, drank a lot of unsweetened green tea, strong and bitter, stimulating his gullet, his gorge, his nostrils.

This tea tasted of awakening.

Wert can't sleep, stretched on the mat spread directly on the ground he listens to the sounds of wind and water, a stream must flow very close by, a spring, the sounds of the river can be faintly heard beneath the clamor of rustling leaves, busy insects travelling all over the wood, the earth, gnawing everything.

His limbs are in some way linked to that nocturnal life, they participate in its movements, the infinitesimal displacements, what's outside him resonates with what's moving within, reassuring or worrying him.

This once bellicose body with its passion for brute force now given up entirely to the flow of life, submitting itself tonight to the programmed degeneration of its cells, feeling their monumental destruction.

Lying down willingly on the coarse bed, casting off the mornings of brightness and noise, the evenings heavy with pride.

The days, the nights of mourning.

Intimate adventure this time, here in this unknown wood at the other end of the world, enclosed in this new landscape.

Sensitive to the connections with this place, the moment they're woven, your body bends to the law of decay and renewal of the flesh, you feel it welcoming the forms around you.

You're living the life of this place and its own physicality, it's your situation now, your relation to the world has been altered by this change, which you believe to be minor; you've been enjoying it for a short while now without being pleased about it, shut away in your fantasy of eternity, your wish for immortality or some form of lunatic survival.

You thought it without admitting it, knew without daring to say it.

And the One over there knows it even better than you!

Who doesn't know it in these parts, doesn't share this knowledge, keep it hidden within him?

The thing that, back where you're from, you'd call a secret, considering it an impossible dream, is simply abolished here, in this night with its murmurs of shadow around you, the murmurs inside you, you who takes the time to listen to and understand it.

The sleepless one got up, made for the door soundlessly, left the cabin.

Found the river path without difficulty, a bed of piled leaves, soon some steps made of stone, an arched bridge of laths, more stones again, and the water below gleaming with rapid flashes between the slats.

The boatman called this short cliff above the water a ledge, the opposite bank is still indistinct, further away than at the level of the estuary perhaps, no lights point it out.

What hamlets might exist on these mountainsides, what peasants, fishermen, the foreigner is enchanted by the mildness of the climate, isn't it still the rainy season?

Crouched on a rock, he waits for a sign, watching the flow of the water, hears little waves hitting the foot of the rock face.

A little later, a vague glow in an ill-defined area of the sky intermittently lights up the barely rippling surface of the river, divides it into skeins where dark brown streaks stand out, branches, or maybe trunks uprooted from the bank.

The glow persists, Wert didn't think the faint and dull light of dawn was so close.

A displaced, tapering form floated past before his eyes to the sea.

Wild, a deadened shadow floating between two layers of waters below.

The dreadful outline breaks against the cliff, the observer, momentarily unsettled, resumes his position once more, a bird's cry makes a bold diagonal fissure through the suddenly cooler, heavier air.

He wonders what this country is, where the first bird of dawn is swooping down onto the water with strong, steadily beating wings, and he lies back more comfortably on the leaves at the edge of the rocks under the incredibly curved branches of the bushes.

That piercing trajectory had, in no time, cleared the way for bird-call of every kind, of every intensity, so diverse that the listener gave up trying to distinguish or compare them, as his ear was always captivated, supplanted at that moment by other calls that sounded more present, even more intriguing.

He couldn't see the birds, was listening to their songs, emitted from innumerable positions staggered along the slope, a resounding flash of sound burst out sometimes, traveled and died out on the opposite shore.

It was less the energy of the calls that captivated his attention than the particularity of their timbre and the complexity of their texture, there a single fine note that didn't sound like a glass bell struck by a beak.

These light, watery sounds spreading out all around would seem suspended for a moment in the humid atmosphere and then would be thrown back again weaker and more distant, endlessly, as though having to travel around the entire earth.

What are you doing there only in a shirt, you're going to catch cold!

A man in conical headgear leaving his features in shadow stands in front of Wert, the black oilskin gives him away.

Let's get going, we're taking the boat out this morning! and the boatman hands Wert his belongings, turns on his heel, is already heading down the basalt stairway.

Rays of light filter through chinks in between the low clouds, the birds have gone quiet, that singing colony, tiny little ones flutter from one tree to the next, throwing out concise notes: announcements or responses.

The path accessing the river makes its way through a fault in the cliff, steps are cut out there, small bare trees, branches bowed at sharp angles, clinging here and there to the patches of glistening rock.

The boat is there right at the bottom on a tongue of sand that takes up almost the whole crevice of the bank, short grass in the surrounding area.

Narrow, very long, stern and prow canted, the two men slide it over the sand and push it gently into the water.

Great calm of the river, not a puff of wind, he can hardly tell that they're saling against the current, mountains following a deeply winding route in the form of a peninsula, perhaps the river is only an arm of sea in an archipelagic maze?

Bistre and brown earth and enclosed light patches, the softened curves of the summits plunge toward the banks, flatten out at the last ledge, straighten out into elongated strips of level ground or short sheer drops of cliff, trees with light foliage on these slender promontories.

Isolated boulders fallen from the cliff face here and there jut out of the fairly shallow water, the boatman maneuvers from one to the next, skirting around obstacles with a silent and sober nonchalance.

Body leaning over, stiff, bent, suspended in the air a short moment, leaning, stiff, repetitive sequence, pole sweeping time into the arc of a perfect circle.

Sitting at the prow of the frail boat, back leaning against the canted stern, the passenger revels in this peaceful progression, fantasy of the explorer discovering a river, going on reconnaissance without thought of danger.

Admires the know-how of the pilot dividing this space in silent strokes, forcing back the air without touching it, supporting himself in order to gain several meters at every thrust of his arms.

Soothed by the pleasant monotony of the cruise, he saw, without worrying about it unduly, the cloudy stratum breaking up little by little and reforming upstream.

When the boatman changes their course slightly at a bend in the river, Wert understands that a different sort of scenery has taken shape on the fringes of his vision, the river has become more meandering without his having noticed, narrower, the landscape standing out more, zones of whitish nebulosity concealing all or part of the slopes.

A tall summit in the distance seems to be detached from its base, remaining suspended up in the sky like the image of a volcano surrounded in mist.

Wert has no trouble convincing himself that the hidden slope of the mountainside enjoys the same features as his immediate surroundings, the lay of the land, the nature of the rocks, the species of trees and flowers.

The idea crosses his mind however that if by some peculiarity of erosion or some ancient cataclysm it was different here, this region would be out of the ordinary.

Xian lives up there, says the boatman, I'll leave you at the bottom.

Wert had assumed that the Master, as secluded as he was from the world, would still reside on the shore or nearby, but to live up there between earth and sky must please him then, he no longer travelled, that was his dwelling place.

Could you see it from here in fair weather?

The newcomer hears the boatman's neutral voice saying that here the weather is always fair, as though this was inarguable, as though this was just one more question too ridiculous to respond to seriously.

After a very tight passage where the two banks were almost touching, the riverbed widened out to the dimensions of a huge lake, lined with rocky outcrops, arched and twisted trees on long projections of sand.

Quite far upstream, Wert thinks he can make out some kinds of cabin, fishermen's houses maybe, this country seems sparsely populated, or maybe the villages are found on the sloped ledges, the folds of the coast inaccessible to the eye.

For a little while longer, the ferryman went on steering the boat with the same accomplished dexterity, making his gestures almost imperceptible, as his passenger tried to spot the location of a pontoon or a pier on the shore, they're so narrow.

At some point, the man relaxed, the boat has come to a standstill between two flat rocks, fitting in exactly, and Wert placed his foot on the firm ground, put his bag on his back.

You follow the path, there are marks here and there, you can't go wrong.

Mission accomplished, the boatman maneuvers backward gracefully to clear this natural landing stage; he finds the flow of the current again, is soon heading back down the river, sinking and hauling on the pole rhythmically without ever lifting his head, which is buried under the vast cone of woven fiber that suits him less than his cap, and even seems to get in his way.

He didn't really seem to be comfortable here.

Beached on the shore, Wert feels more isolated than lonely in the diffuse light and the heavy heat, he's hungry, hasn't eaten anything since the day before, was the fasting part of this ritual approach?

The Master is waiting for him up there, but waiting for him which day?

Standing on the makeshift pontoon, he feels a great weariness, all the fatigue accumulated on those stages of his journey beset by risks and dangers floods back at once and lands on the nape of his neck, makes its way painfully down the length of his spine, poor exhausted wretch, broken, has difficulty getting up, sitting on the rock where he landed just a few moments before.

Sees himself unkempt, dirty, beard and hair disheveled, clothes stained and torn, his hardened skin leathery from the sun, the surf, the months of ordeal and of labor at sea.

The boatman and his pole have already slipped away into the straits downstream between the narrow channel between those two banks, you couldn't see a living soul on the opposite shore, distant at present, the seeming absence of settlements almost a cause for concern.

Recurrent dizzy spells hit the traveler in silent waves, dissolution of the adventure or darkening of its resolution, diffuse evanescence of its action, of the tension of his mind, of the project that built up that tension and kept him on the alert.

Isn't it insulting to your vigilance to falter like this, to your persistence to doubt like this, to your curiosity, this innate gift of the nomad within the city?

Have you had to beg the secret from the Master? he whispered it to you last night, whispered it in your ear without your expecting it, you only have to reconnect the knowledge contained in your body to that which is present here in the mutating bodies surrounding and comforting yours.

How long does he remain there prostrate, stricken by this bleak lifelessness, denying the achievement of the immense journey through which he's just lived?

Dozed off no doubt in the glare reflected from above, brooding over his weakness, calling himself unattractive names, he couldn't say where they'd come from, catch-all terms for his evasion, for this self-indulgence, which is hardly his best trait.

At some point, his disinclination slid away into the course of the water bathing his feet, resuscitating his pleasure in observing the things surrounding him.

A bird with a very long beak and a tail plumed with pink feathers landed a short distance away in a creek, he followed it with his eyes as it took flight again, he got up, considered anew the mountainside he had to climb, planted with strange, twisted trees, started walking over black earth and pebbles.

The path follows a muddy border at the edge of some reeds, winds between tall stalks with white fuzz that brushes his face, moves away a little farther from the banks, passes onto firm ground, a path for a single human being, narrow and slippery, makes its way between two beds where streams are cascading down.

Unable to hold out anymore, dripping with sweat, the parched traveler kneels, greedily swallows a swig of cold water.

The rocky masses on the mountainside are completely different from those he caught sight of from the boat, towering up vertically with smooth surfaces and becoming rounded at the summit, supporting one another, joined together in places with a shared impetus, continuous, irrepressible, on either side of the small valley.

Remains of dismantled cabins appear at a bend, thatched or sloping wooden roofs, you couldn't tell beneath the accumulation of dead branches and thorn bushes.

Ancient region, these ruins and their state of abandonment, the path penetrates further into a gorge with walls close to touching, region with long-lasting traces, indelible.

Did those collapsed huts present an enigma to walkers from times past as well? Wert wonders in an attack of geographical sentiment as exempt from romanticism as from nostalgia.

The trees intrigue him, to what species do they belong, conifers viewed from a distance, but the trunks soon seem jagged, the contorted branches flung out in every direction make Wert abandon this term and every other known to him.

Obtuse angles at the first elbows, arms flung out distortedly at every point of the horizon, the distance from the vertical narrows at the approach to the summit, the general appearance is of a confused system of split and bristly branches.

In a passage with a steep slope where some steps have been carved out, uneven, broken up, a man tears down toward him, dressed in a short, brown pelisse.

His back to the rock, the climber struggles to step aside, the man brushing past him gives him a wink then takes up his hell-for-leather pace once more, disappears into the fog rising on the mountainside.

The big river and its opposite bank are now invisible, all the country downstream as far as the sea.

In front of him, fumarolic gases are sliding over the surface of the wall, hiding all mineral, vegetal, and human forms, a bitter cold beats down on the land; frozen, Wert wraps himself up hurriedly.

He has entered the white zone that cuts into the summit of the mountain, wasn't expecting it yet, doesn't know at what moment he entered it.

There were plenty of other abrupt ramps and shelves in the rock, the path through this extremely compartmentalized terrain was frequently changing course.

An observer positioned on the opposite shore would have been able to reconstruct his climb, connecting up in his mind the visible sections begun right or left and then cut off cleanly by the cloudbank spiriting everything from view.

Here, however, the thick clouds didn't form a mass that was all of one piece, uniformly dense, instead they circulated at varying speeds, separated, frayed; at irregular intervals between those diaphanous ribbons the landscape reformed little by little before the unruffled visitor's eyes.

It was no longer made up of those twisted figures of prickly trees with their dead or withered branches, but of mountain trees, firs, larches, and in the well-sheltered areas there were quinces, walnuts, flowers of every hue on the ground, like a spring print colored in with whatever came to hand.

A case of pencils at random.

Tiled roofs could be partially seen between the huge trunks that were surrounded by a powdery mist, a chimney was smoking.

On this still slightly sloping area where, from all sides, the white vapors were spreading, a special atmosphere prevailed, invigorating, almost burning the lungs, stimulating the worn-out cycle of breath.

The weight of his body diminished, his stride became brisk, longer than usual, the amused traveler felt a gratifying elasticity at play in his muscles.

Followed a meadow that was spongy in places, a river was overflowing, pools spread on the path itself, their water lukewarm to the touch.

Was this the world of Xian and his people, this secret place as though plucked from some other peaceful location and transplanted here after a decision to distance themselves, wanting nothing more than to retreat?

As mobile and changeable as were its texture and form, the cloud never entirely cleared the upper regions of the mountain, the cliffs must keep this place isolated, hemmed in, Wert mused, cliffs carved from faults, pitted with grottos.

That last word was the right one, grotto more than cave, he soon made out the first excavation worthy of that mythic name between the trees.

The first grotto seems abandoned, barely unblocked, narrow, a hedge of brambles obstructing the entrance.

From the second, on hearing footsteps, a small child dressed in a skimpy pelisse comes out, he stations himself on the threshold, considers the stranger, whose big bag makes him laugh.

In the third, the fourth, only some sheep who become alarmed, lying on straw, bleating in turn with the same plaintive, unjustified cry, they're comfortable and well fed.

Nobody in the next two, neither of them with very large mouths, a man would have difficulty slipping inside.

Sitting on a threshing floor in front of the entrance to the seventh, a little boy with a shaved head is stumbling through an alphabet book, he spells aloud at the top of his voice, each well-articulated letter rings out in the evening air, floats there for a time, disappears with a sudden crack, as though sucked into the grotto's interior.

With a greeting slipped between two letters, the newcomer signals his presence, the boy raises his eyes, immediately stands up.

It's you who's searching for Xian? follow me, he lives nearby.

It wasn't far, in fact the eighth grotto was the right one, its entrance carved with a lowered curve, worn down in places, numerous pieces of stone had become detached from it over the course of time.

The Master would like to inform you that he's doing his exercises, please settle in here while waiting for him.

He was pointing out a very old and very worn deep-pile rug, its colors faded, still reasonably well suited to taking a nap.

Wert sat down there, at the foot of a small tree, a cherry no doubt, a partial darkness had settled over the plateau, the cloud seemed contracted, shrunk in on itself, there was no longer any light filtering between its swirls, which were eddying far less than they had been in the afternoon under the sun.

Found he was completely at ease, wedged against the trunk of the tree, and contrary to what he'd feared the air was warming up bit by bit, the irregularities of this atypical climate must wear off with the coming of night.

Had been so hungry all day long that the desire to eat had left him.

Wondered how long the Master's exercises would last.

Interrogated himself in recurring snatches as to his intentions with regard to him, the questioning got lost in a maze of evasive propositions with haphazard syntax.

In the middle of the dark night, a reddish glow at the entrance to the grotto wakes him.

Why on earth light a fire, is it the custom here, the logs are already burning, would he really have slept so long?

A spasm in his stomach, weakened aftershock of the attack back at the Twins, returns him for a moment to that distant scene, his leg throbs a bit too, what had he known at that stage about the end of his journey?

His body healed, barely a mark to be seen any longer from that creature's impossible route, finds himself in the same position, though not against the rock now, a fruit tree is fitting for this new phase.

Sound of a stream or river close by, a bird in the depths of the meadow hoots in sonorous accompaniment, smells of sap, of dead wood, and those creatures under the earth and at ground level, persevering and struggling, slaving away, wasting away, coming undone, decomposing, and the leaves, the branches.

Wilted flowers, molted buds.

Is it you who is here, warrior of so many years, years that were only one day?

Pressing his ear to the ground, he listens to the tremendous, unceasing bustle of the creatures' activity, scratching, crawling, rummaging, foraging in the soil, devouring, tearing to shreds, masticating, reconstructing the earth.

Creatures evading his gaze, in the lens of the magnifying glass between eye and broken ground, excavations, the microscopic hollows making up the path.

Blood of the earth into the earth spilled spurting, blood from the arteries beating with an erratic rhythm, at intervals echoing time, intimate dependency.

Wert feels this symbiosis in his heart, belonging to the same order of things digging through the earth.

To violate it isn't worth it.

At some point, the blanket of cloud parted, he saw the stars, the bluish patches on the grassy surfaces between the shadows of the trunks, the lunar glittering in the foliage.

A light wind blew in and muted the nocturnal sounds of the earth.

Wert got up, walked, a thing among beings, he bathed, washed in the river.

Went back to sleep under the tree.

I tested your patience, your willingness, appreciated your calm, your silence too.

The man in the white tunic towers over him, enormous, immersing his eyes in Wert's own as he lies on the ground at the foot of the cherry tree.

Come, I'm going to teach you my exercises.

He leads Wert toward this crevice in the cliff that is his dwelling-place, cave, and retreat.

Standing up, Wert saw that the Master wasn't taller than he was at all, stocky and strong, his head shaved.

Had enough time to notice the ashen fringes of dawn to the east.

Still not really awake, entered the grotto, all the heat from the Master's nocturnal fire is somehow kept inside, magnifying itself, it was bright inside, brighter than he imagined, a glow emanated from the rock face, a radiance owing to some characteristic of the rock, to a rare substance hidden in its veins.

But a soft light, too weak for reading but not for writing, sufficient for handling objects, for getting around without mishap.

These pleasant surprises diverted the newcomer from observing his host, he suddenly finds himself facing him, face clean-shaven and round, short nose, thin lips, black eyes without any particular sparkle, lowered now rather than staring at this stranger.

Wert took in his steady voice, its ordinary register, enunciating without effect, without affect.

Welcome to my home, I thought you would be taller, we're going to do the movements for the coming of the dawn together, pay attention, do your best, my name is Master.

Very well, Master.

Take off your old clothes, put on these sandals, make yourself comfortable.

The purpose of this session is to deepen one's breathing, Wert applies himself, overtaken by events, caught unprepared, torn between prescribed observation of the Master's movements and concealed furtive observation of his face.

The first task consists of a series of twistings of the torso and of bendings of the knees, to be held for varying lengths of time depending on the phase of breathing, of the holding or letting go of the breath.

We will see other combinations of this kind, the Master comments after a time, the variations are infinite, some of them demand a lot of the novice little accustomed to regulating his respiratory function, to controlling it at length, bending it to his will.

And all this time, the student fails to glimpse on Xian's face the subterfuge he thought he'd find there.

A subsequent exercise allows Wert to examine the Master's features more easily and from nearer by, the two men are standing up, torsos bent, palms flattened on the thighs, after taking a deep breath, they have to remain in apnea for as long as they can stand the burning.

Wert is at leisure then to note that the skin of the person opposite, surprisingly smooth on the forehead and cheeks, becomes wrinkled at his temples and chin; that, not very creased on the back of the hands, it shrivels on the phalanges, as though gnarled, sclerosed perhaps.

The Master's eyes reveal nothing more than two points of an undefined glimmer, simple organs of vision, no hint there of all the things that can touch and animate the spirit, there is neither feeling nor idea in them, the extreme tension of his body in this posture no doubt makes them look like that.

The total absence of eyebrows is quite embarrassing for others.

After this seemingly endless strain, the Master exhales the entire volume of inhaled air with a violent and noisy discharge, bends the nape of his neck, relaxes, cancels his meditation with his entire being.

The novice, close to collapsing, held out well, his mass of contaminated air as though trapped inside his skull escapes from his throat in a prolonged groan, he chokes, collapses, kneels to the ground.

Stand up, that's not bad for a beginning, you'll have to calm your nerves; this evening we will meditate at the hour of Vacuity of the Bodies.

The Master points out a straw mattress with dwarf-palm fibers provided as a pillow, a water pitcher, an unbleached linen towel, Wert reaches the bed staggering, wipes off the sweat streaming over his whole body, gets his breath back with difficulty.

Shortly afterward, two servants make their entrance, an old man burdened with a pitcher and a tray, a youth with a new pelisse in the newcomer's size.

His skin is adapting itself to the fluctuations of the climate here, put that on and be seated, I hope you're hungry now, Xian adds, inviting his student to share this substantial refreshment to break their fast.

Though he finds the rustic garment pleasant to wear, a persistent pain in his lungs prevents Wert from enjoying the food as much as he wants to, he has difficulty swallowing, finds it hard to see, the light from outside, bright at present, makes that inside the grotto seem pale.

The meal consists of a vegetable soup, of rice and dried fish, apples, dates, spring water, and green tea without sugar.

He eats it in silence, Wert disciplines his throat, his stomach, his hands, eats as slowly as he can, savors the food, drinks a lot of very cool water, a little tea.

Furtively eyes the Master who barely touches the food, leans back often on his cushion, his eyes gazing at the apex of the roof, the differentiated patches on his face seem superimposed, the transitions so barely noticeable that the guest fails every time to find a common point of ageing or rejuvenation between them.

Grayish skin, white in places, in others veined with rosacea.

Ageless, this cliché passes through his mind, overused, without life, renunciation of the words that would penetrate the mystery.

Black eyes suddenly piercing, staring at the other, even if they lack expression.

We don't want for anything, you see, the seasons here overlap, the cloud makes miracles, its powers at work have a thousand ways of manifesting themselves, they renew our energy at every moment.

And he gets up, gestures for Wert to follow him.

His entire body worn-out, Wert rises with difficulty, severity of the exercises or weight of the years, no longer feels as animated as he did at the beginning of his journey, consequence of his ordeals, of the nights of poor sleep.

Acute sensation of what had been inside him one evening, he pushed it far away from himself so violently that whole night long.

They went out into the great outdoors, reached a fringe of the plateau taken over by impenetrable nebulous matter swirling around and drifting toward the lower slopes.

In the densest layers, the distant forms of trees rallied suddenly, standing up before them, and those of docile cattle grazing alone, as though having marked their territory once and for all, never to wander.

With his first steps, Wert felt that elasticity of muscle once more that had so struck him the day before, it reduced his cramps and aches in no time at all, every stride was now only a light spring on the grass.

Xian, strangely, walked with an irregular step, now scurrying, now elongating his gait outrageously, seemed jovial for the past few moments, was more talkative.

The cloud on the mountainside often falls away early in the morning, you see the whole valley, one time I saw the sea.

Surprised by this confidence, the newcomer becomes bolder, asks if you can make out the coast to the west.

I don't see it, I hear it, the forester, the canteen lady spoke to me about you, I've been following you since the Twins.

The Master also says that he'd heard of Wert's other exploits as well, of his sorrow, never doubting his resolve, but doubting his success, many in the past have attempted the journey in vain.

What they say about me where you're from doesn't always make sense, they find it hard to guess right, I'll explain it to you bit by bit, we have the time, the truth will come out along the way.

They followed the edge of the plateau, couldn't see the summit of the mountain, the cloudy white region is disconnected from the summit, its domain is the mid-slope, in-between place, of confrontation, area of awakening and new direction.

Xian had come to a halt a little further on in front of a tuft of thistles, purple flowers barely open, it's just here that the path begins, he said then, only the messenger, you passed him didn't you? knows the place, it's impossible to find again.

The idea doesn't even occur to you, he added in a murmur.

The words had occurred to him, at least.

The cloud parted and they saw a planting of larches a bit further below, some had lost their leaves, others hadn't, further down again firs, palms, birches, the two men contemplated the mountainside for a moment, the cloud poured back together again, they turned around and walked away.

Then the children arrived in a group, the birds and the children.

About thirty in number.

Running dementedly through the mist with the birds surrounding them, flying right over their heads, swooping down and beating their wings over them trying to find their way between these obstacles.

You'd almost think that the objective of the birds' little game is to divide and then round the children up again in a different way, to prevent them from gathering and then force them to regroup and play together once more.

The children, however, seem to play according to their own arrangements, barely paying attention to the schemes of their feathered friends, especially because they're aware of the intention that could be attributed to them.

At one point, all the birds form a circle over their heads, now gathered almost fortuitously at a single point, and whether by chance or not, everyone holds this position for a brief moment, then they all scatter with a single impetus, between the trees, beyond the trees.

Their dances are improvised, Xian explains, now it's the children, now the birds who give the signal.

Wert has seen some of those birds before, their wings shimmered with glistening gray during their spiral flight, with a brilliant ruby color in their vertical ascent, it was a country of creeping wind and of dust.

High-pitched shouts from the children, shrill ones from the birds, which are mimicking the others, or parodying them, simulating them?

He sees the pack in their little white tunics again, changing position unceasingly and running so quickly between the trees that he's unable to keep track of them.

The fleecy swirls of mist spirit them from view for a moment, some reappeared in the same place, others seemed to have leaped much further away in the meantime, these movements happening outside of time, pulled off without a single accident or fall in spite of everything, were beginning to hurt his eyes, he covered them as though to drown out those intermittent, sparkling, excessively colored projections.

And the children, could they see him?

You'll get used to it, Xian says as he sets off walking again, you'll see more and more easily through the mist, they have no problem seeing you.

The newcomer, intrigued by everything in this disconcerting place, notices how clear the Master's voice is at that moment, how precise his diction; at other times it gushes out of his throat with a rumble, his lips filtering down the sound until it becomes steady, a little hoarse.

They went along the river, reached the waterfall, a gigantic casuarina towers over the waterfall, other birds are nesting there, small and white, they twitter, chatter, so numerous that you can no longer see the branches.

Further below, the stream is divided by stages and sweeps of it disappear between the rocks, farther away than the cloud allows the eye to see.

Xian will remain there a long while contemplating the waterfall, head cocked, as though listening to a reedy voice or whispering to his novice that this is the opportunity to question, to manifest his desire to learn, to really adapt to the life of the region.

The nights, Master, and the days here, the other will ask, are they the same length as those of the outside world?

Xian, impassive, will respond that if the lengths do differ to a large extent, considering the local particularities, the relation of one's body to this event, like that of the event to time, remain more or less similar.

A silence will fall, Wert doesn't seem to have grasped the full significance of these words, Xian will make himself more clear.

How long do you think your journey lasted?

Ten days, Master, fifteen maybe.

A year! Xian the Sage will announce, and a quick streak of cloud will surge by all at once, will envelope the traveler's body and mind, will drown his certitudes, his reference points, the foundations of his knowledge, his understanding.

He'll revisit the interminable hours he spent ascending the pass, those of his stay at the top, impossible to measure, in the glacial cold and with the worry, that strange impression he had in the gap between the peaks of having walked so little to cover such a great distance.

The fluctuating space that evening in the canteen, the inconsistency of the length of the storm at sea.

The Master seems to be looking at him disinterestedly once more, his expression sullen, distant, no doubt disappointed that the novice hadn't noticed this incredible disjunction and discrepancy till now.

Wert will think that Xian wants to test his judgment, his capacity to interpret new sensations correctly, his composure perhaps, or simply his credulity.

Will think that what was said is true.

Unhinged, paralyzed in an outmoded sphere of life, he will walk like a shadow at the Master's side, cross a wooden bridge, enter cultivated fields, plots of earth planted with barley, corn, broad beans, will cross them no longer knowing in what part of his mind they grow.

Will come to an abrupt halt, stare at the Master in a kind of confusion, pose a word that will remain between his lips.

Will find himself out of his depth, caught in a scene with multiple figures, duplicates, they'll feign distress, fear, and his body will crumble, dissolve, he'll no longer be aware of anything but his hands, a semblance of hands.

This place contains its own pretenses, he'll say in a toneless voice, they themselves contain him, he himself . . .

Text strung together off the cuff, error on the tablet.

This new place is plausible enough, Xian stays close to the novice, the people from the hamlet keep their distance a little, they don't form a circle but are lined up in front of a log building, rakes, pickaxes in hand, pale and brown pelisses swap places incessantly, groups split apart, impermanent, the cloud divides them, there are perhaps fifty of them, or a hundred.

A glimmer passes across the Master's gray eyes at that moment, women and men are becoming animated, offering greetings perhaps, gestures interrupted by caesura, the children are absent, still off running around, the birds beaded with pink spinning above them.

Sickles, sheaves, it's harvest time, says Xian, elsewhere they're plowing, we have all the vegetables, all the fruit we want, all year long, if that word doesn't still alarm you.

There must be seven or eight thatched cottages, some buildings with tile roofs, a cowshed, a henhouse, some goats appear, bleating between the onlookers, slip away, some guinea pigs.

Sections of wall stand at unpredictable points over the mountainside, and large oaks, pepper trees, elms.

The elm here doesn't die, you see, no Dutch elm disease.

Thick hair falling over their shoulders, chestnut curls on the men, very pale women with jet-black braids.

Wert is struck by the paleness of their faces, a result of the screen of mist? he must also appear pale; is his skin changing, already looking different?

For how long has he been standing in front of these people, now?

A girl approaches him, or a boy, presents him with a basket carefully filled with dates, olives, recites a little speech, the newcomer has trouble catching it, these people are definitely using a dialect, all or most of it escapes him.

The majority have been here a lot longer than me, says Xian to Wert's surprise, I never understand more than a handful of what they're saying, they make the words up as they go along.

The flavor of the fruits gives the visitor an appetite, the little ceremony has touched him deeply, he'd like to thank them, but a shifting of the wind conceals the participants' features, erases the houses, the trees.

Master Xian led him, making his way through the fog as though by divination, an ancient practice says the one who has just been accepted into this world to himself, not knowing how he can benefit from his emotion.

The ground is rising slightly, we're following the river, it's not very wide here, watch where you put your feet!

On the brink of falling into the water, the newcomer clings to the smooth trunk of a fig tree, this is our orchard, explains the Master, apple trees, pear trees, further on mango trees, lychee trees, only the kiwi trees won't adapt to the region, I wonder why not, *you* ought to know that.

Flowers all over the hill, poppies, primroses, a wisteria creeping in luminescent clusters across the mist.

They emerged from the thick of the cloud, stopped at the spring, the water bubbling out of a cavern between two limestone strata, the bluish-gray of the rock glistening in the half-light.

Midday, let's go a little higher, Xian says, it's time for the Vacuity of the Bodies.

On a grassy mound emerging momentarily from the mist, he sits down, hands on his knees, looks straight ahead in the direction of the invisible valley, in this way he intermittently overlooks the cloud safeguarding the permanence of his domain.

It's not his domain, this domain belongs to everyone, anyone who wishes to may come here and settle, the traveler has witnessed that, actor as much as witness of course, his whole life would be held between those two terms.

He came of his own free will to the unhappy surprise of his people, the novelty of the journey molded his feelings and thoughts into other shapes, that brutal hero's past doesn't belong to him anymore, the word for immortality isn't understood by the ears of this country as it was in the glorious heart of his distant headquarters.

He won't be made immortal here through his body as he had been through his exploits back there.

But in another manner he will be, in another matter.

In the meantime, he sat down to the left of the Master, took up the same posture as him, eyes like his held on the uncertain world beyond the cloud.

One doesn't need to be in privileged surroundings in order to find the void within, Wert muses, though it seemed to him that it must be more difficult to detach oneself from one's trivial circumstances in ugliness and noise than it would be in some enchanting setting, though here everything is so pleasant that he actually has great difficulty in cutting himself off from it.

Nothing is exteriorized in this kind of exercise, a spectator would watch in vain for any sign, the body of the performer unfailingly displays only a disarming stillness, adheres to a private procedure not betrayed by any gesture.

The neophyte is willing, maintains his position, waiting for the Master to give him advice, but the Master has forgotten him, has included him in the set of things to exclude from his sphere.

So, he must apply himself to not thinking of anything, he thinks, to chasing off every alarming or worrying subject, he allows his body to bathe in the misty transparency of non-action.

At one point, he feels he's no longer there, he's on the other side of self and is observing himself, then he occupies himself with driving away the observer for a time, feels himself there once again, has to begin all over again.

Nothing works as well as that morning's exercises for inhaling, exhaling, and mastering the changeable volume of one's breath, the effort of regulation links his mind so closely to the immediate future of the phenomena from which he is failing to free himself.

Xian will teach him, will initiate him into his techniques, he'd been so little trained in these matters as a child.

The cloud is moving, gradually spreading higher up, so dense now that the two men seated on the mound searching for the path to a complete knowledge of the world become isolated from one another.

Path of listening, of hearing pure sounds, purity, origins, words that the apprentice pilgrim never heard where he's from, he's wary of them.

Do they have meaning here?

He stares intensely at the cloud and it's at the heart of this haziness that the void perceptibly forms, here potentialities diversify, clash, combine, the invisible forces attach to one another and come apart, they test expected forms and their way of coming into existence.

Their way of evolving in the minutes to come.

In the hours, the years to come in this marginal place where units for measuring time are nonexistent, its secret will lie in the absence of unity.

Except for the unity of the world.

At the end of a perceived length of time lacking any punctuation in the white void that had sprung up in his ears, the newcomer sits up straight, sees the Master who's watching him with curiosity.

Are you coming back from such a long way off, so captivated by what you've heard?

Surprised by these words, the novice senses a certain irony in them, you're coming back down to earth is what they say where he's from.

They both get up at the same moment, contemplate the twisting display overhanging the cloud one last time, for how long has this non-meditation on the nothing of things gone on?

The most difficult part is quieting the voice, Xian will say on the descent, I don't always succeed in that, I must admit.

They paused at the spring, drank from its eddy, the disciple found the water a little too warm for his taste, the Master savored it or pretended to.

A narrow path led directly from the mound back to the grottos, the orchard to their right, the absence of trees on this route leaving it free of hazards.

At one point the path passed by an opening way up above, difficult to access, archway covered in loose stones and shells, sanctuary or crypt depending on the century, what sort of history does this country have?

What does history mean here?

At what point did Xian arrive, was he born here?

Miraculously saved from the great flood, alone, destitute, cave-dwelling ancestor crouching in his den, memory-guardian of the selection, of this gift from the All-Powerful figures of legend?

A stocky man with a long, brown mane of hair is waiting at the foot of the cherry tree, scissors and brushes, razors and creams in a little case under his arm, gets up nimbly at their approach.

With a sign, the Master leaves his companion in the man's hands, leaving the barber to liberate the other of his knotted and dirty hair, of his reddish-gray and unremarkable beard.

Leaves the man to dress him in an off-white tunic similar to the Master's, loose-fitting, no doubt too loose-fitting for he who has weakened so much in the course of his long journey.

Now you are well attired, says Xian on seeing him cross the threshold, this garment is light, similar to the pelisse, you'll be comfortable in it, and your thoughts will be freer too.

He's in the process of handling some phials, tubes, various substances in jars around him, what elixir is he preparing?

Man of the Mountain is my other name, he tells you that long life requires knowledge, invention, enthusiasm, you have to learn and learn more, polish the seed of the soul, motion without friction need never cease.

The newly chosen one is intrigued by these preparations, he is unfamiliar with alchemy, external or otherwise, observes the Master concentrating, eyes closed, as though going back over the formulas on an inverted table.

The light in the grotto, pale, very pale even, surprises Wert a little, did they stay up there the whole afternoon meditating or striving to no longer do so?

Your senses are deceiving you, it's true, but less than reason has, much less than speech, than language even.

He who has come from so far to meet the sage and seek his secret is here now in his dwelling place beside he who accepts him, companion and disciple; he will share his life, learn much from him, will carry on his name, his legacy.

A secret that isn't meant for those from this place, so little like what those from outside believe.

Meanwhile, the Master has filled two bowls with a bluish-green mixture, his is handed to him with extreme care.

Drink that in small sips, it will invigorate you, you're strong, you're only around thirty after all.

You were only around thirty when you entered this isolated world from which you can't leave, not that the idea even occurs to you, Xian was saying, was it misleading to mention a number that no longer has significance once you've passed a certain point?

Sitting cross-legged on his straw mattress, holding the receptacle with both hands, the young disciple drinks with caution the drug sweetened so as to remove the bitterness and which makes his throat so sticky.

The taste brings to his mind a plant from his country, acaulescent gentian with its beautiful blue flower, or villarsia, menyanthaceae.

Ensconced on his cushion, Xian savors the familiar potion, at that moment his height seemed difficult to determine, problematic to describe, confusing for the mind in this rocky and strangely not very damp den, filled with a greenish luminosity as the unpredictable light outside—distinguishing trees, livestock, the river and the inhabitants of the hamlet all day long—fades.

Positioned there in good humor, legs folded under him on his pallet, which is spread out on the ground, the curve of the arching wall allows him, if he leans back slightly, to rest his head against it from time to time.

In this posture, his double chin disappears, his lips fill out, eyes widen, seem farther apart all of sudden, even glowing now.

This plant grows beside the sea, he explains, setting the empty bowl down again on the rattan table that connects the two men and separates them as well, gathering it is not without its risks, a snake keeps watch over the murky water.

To drink this modest quantity of liquid at this time when the light is changing seems to give him unlimited satisfaction, every concern reaches an acceptable level, equal in gravity and urgency.

You'll explain to me, about the kiwis?

He's picking his bowl up again, lapping up the few remaining drops, his fingers stroking the rough terra cotta, the legs of the cooking tripod, the lovely light brown glaze.

I used to have the knack, I was the one who turned these bowls, I like making things, there's nothing like it to give you confidence, you develop a sort of savoir-faire because you know how to move your hands with accuracy, your fingers learn more quickly and better than you to know the material you're working with, better than the words you use to analyze and dissect it.

The place is as bright now as a bedroom or office in which to read and write, here where there's neither books nor paper on which to write, no stamp or stylus for cutting into or carving the rock.

The novice feels something like lines taking shape on his skin, sees those on the Master's skin changing, runs his fingers over his own cheeks, his nose, the skin at the nape of his neck, his ears.

What noticeable changes had his time in this place already worked on him, a time neither reliable nor verifiable, without a clear gauge?

Impossible to compare the time in the world he came from and the time in this world, time without reference points, which can no longer called time perhaps but a fundamental space, ancient, sheltering each pulse beneath its wing.

Take leave of your habitual mannerisms and reactions, stop feeling yourself, scratching your face, says Xian, watching him do it, leave your skin to follow the flow of things, same as you, part of the same motion.

Some amount of time later, depending on how much time was stretched, no doubt encouraged by the mixture, Xian will continue, in a short while we will do the evening exercises, and soon all this will seem like gold to you, compared to the lexicon you've always held so dear.

Needless to say we haven't any mirrors here.

He went quiet and, tilting his head backward, contemplated the arched roof where the sparkling of the mica over the whole surface of the rock created a slender sort of dome of white light, it looked as though tiny insects were swirling around there, thrown into turmoil by the brightness.

He remained motionless and silent for an indefinite period of time, so long that he seemed to have fallen into something like sleep, wide-open black eyes observing something above him in a dream that intrigued and enchanted him.

The younger man, there as company, felt at one point that the unusual mixture was once again substantially boosting his strength, the incredibly diverse worlds into which he was now advancing often seemed to him to succeed one another seamlessly, and sometimes to join or fit together too quickly for him to be able to grasp the chain of events and learn from it.

Space in some sense was contracting before his very eyes, he thought, from the world of his childhood to this white zone and grotto and the body in the grotto experiencing this phenomenon; but in another sense it had expanded even more quickly.

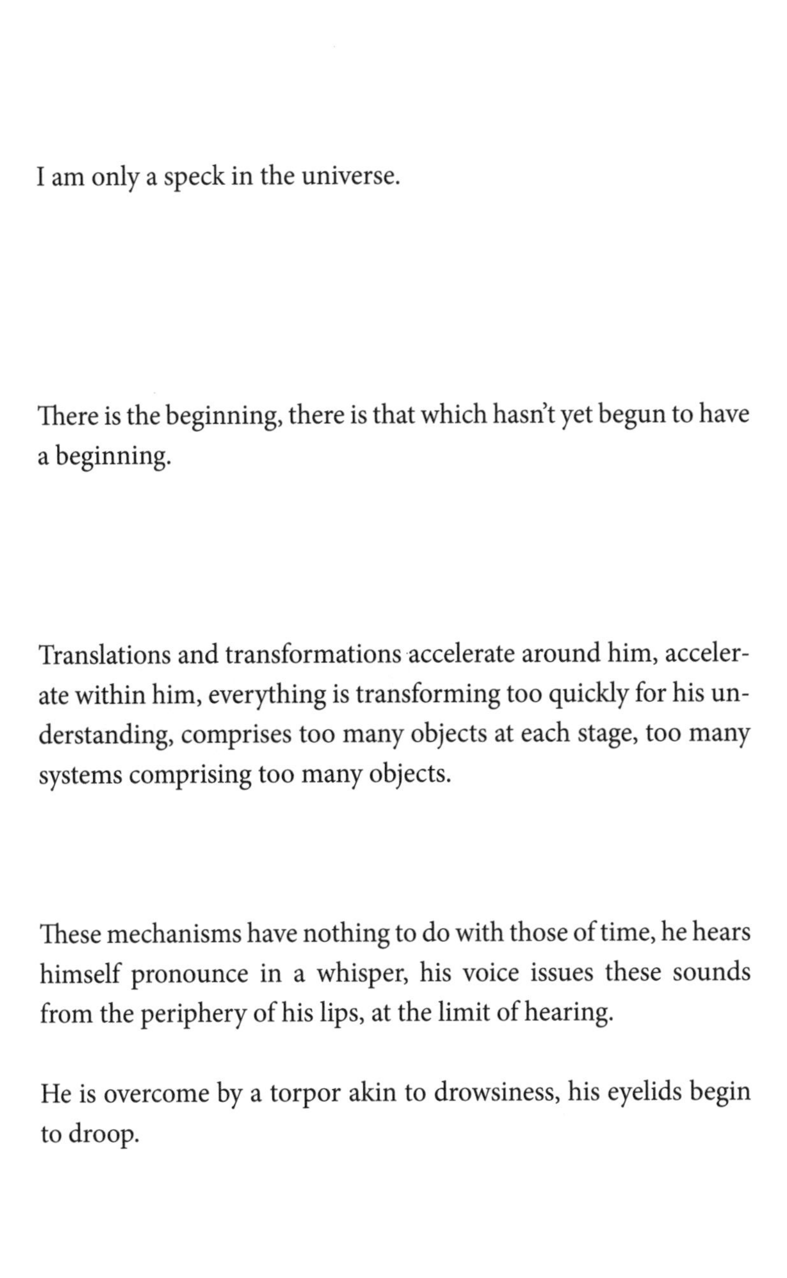

I am only a speck in the universe.

There is the beginning, there is that which hasn't yet begun to have a beginning.

Translations and transformations accelerate around him, accelerate within him, everything is transforming too quickly for his understanding, comprises too many objects at each stage, too many systems comprising too many objects.

These mechanisms have nothing to do with those of time, he hears himself pronounce in a whisper, his voice issues these sounds from the periphery of his lips, at the limit of hearing.

He is overcome by a torpor akin to drowsiness, his eyelids begin to droop.

This grotto, the opposite of headquarters, its underground passages perhaps.

Hall of destinies, reading the past anew from the tablets.

Black is the color outside, nothing registers on this black that's stretched out like a screen, though outside the river is flowing, causing fluctuations in the walls of mist.

For how long have you lived here?

(Is it Xian who spoke?)

A breeze like a wind that's lost its way gently brushes past the threshold of the cave.

The thudding of unhurried clogs, striking the grass of the field between the phantom trees coming to meet the morning, hamlet too far away to be able to hear his people, laughing, crying.

Days drawn out, priceless, outside the circle of the inevitable.

The Master still seems distracted, savoring the taste of his brew.

Whispers a word, something bothers him, leaves him, bothers him again.

We're going to have to find you a name!

Is this a piece of advice, an order? to whom does it fall to find the name?

The newcomer in his sleepiness thinks he can make out a glow in the nearby undergrowth, a wave borne by a weak tide outlining the shadow of a garden, the shadow of a path lined with yew trees and of an apple tree, of a well.

And black is no longer the color outside: the moon is full at present.

Bluish aura.

And this long, white rectangle on the sand at the threshold of the grotto.

He feels himself get up, move toward the threshold.

To remain on the edge of this incursion of whiteness that was spread out like chalk dust over the sand.

The word incursion is in keeping with the unpredictability of the moment: he wasn't expecting such an obstacle, that's all.

His legs wouldn't take the plunge, that's all there was to it.

Then he crosses the threshold and goes into the garden.

Goes around the well, stumbles over the field of stones, the stones take up all the space between the gate and the apple tree.

A great many stones piled up and scattered across the way.

Then he goes through the gate and runs down the path and lifts the stones one by one and throws them to the right, to the left, hard as he can.

CLAUDE OLLIER, one of the major forces behind the nouveau roman and recipient of several prestigious literary awards, including the Prix Médecis, is the author of more than twenty books of fiction, drama, memoir, and criticism.

URSULA MEANY SCOTT is a literary translator from French and Spanish. She holds an MPhil in literary translation from Trinity College, Dublin, and her translations have appeared in two volumes of the *Best European Fiction* series to date.

SELECTED DALKEY ARCHIVE PAPERBACKS

Petros Abatzoglou, *What Does Mrs. Freeman Want?*
Michal Ajvaz, *The Golden Age.*
The Other City.
Pierre Albert-Birot, *Grabinoulor.*
Yuz Aleshkovsky, *Kangaroo.*
Felipe Alfau, *Chromos.*
Locos.
Ivan Ângelo, *The Celebration.*
The Tower of Glass.
David Antin, *Talking.*
António Lobo Antunes, *Knowledge of Hell.*
Alain Arias-Misson, *Theatre of Incest.*
Iftikhar Arif and Waqas Khwaja, eds., *Modern Poetry of Pakistan.*
John Ashbery and James Schuyler, *A Nest of Ninnies.*
Gabriela Avigur-Rotem, *Heatwave and Crazy Birds.*
Heimrad Bäcker, *transcript.*
Djuna Barnes, *Ladies Almanack.*
Ryder.
John Barth, *LETTERS.*
Sabbatical.
Donald Barthelme, *The King.*
Paradise.
Svetislav Basara, *Chinese Letter.*
René Belletto, *Dying.*
Mark Binelli, *Sacco and Vanzetti Must Die!*
Andrei Bitov, *Pushkin House.*
Andrej Blatnik, *You Do Understand.*
Louis Paul Boon, *Chapel Road.*
My Little War.
Summer in Termuren.
Roger Boylan, *Killoyle.*
Ignácio de Loyola Brandão, *Anonymous Celebrity.*
The Good-Bye Angel.
Teeth under the Sun.
Zero.
Bonnie Bremser, *Troia: Mexican Memoirs.*
Christine Brooke-Rose, *Amalgamemnon.*
Brigid Brophy, *In Transit.*
Meredith Brosnan, *Mr. Dynamite.*
Gerald L. Bruns, *Modern Poetry and the Idea of Language.*
Evgeny Bunimovich and J. Kates, eds., *Contemporary Russian Poetry: An Anthology.*
Gabrielle Burton, *Heartbreak Hotel.*
Michel Butor, *Degrees.*
Mobile.
Portrait of the Artist as a Young Ape.
G. Cabrera Infante, *Infante's Inferno.*
Three Trapped Tigers.
Julieta Campos, *The Fear of Losing Eurydice.*
Anne Carson, *Eros the Bittersweet.*
Orly Castel-Bloom, *Dolly City.*
Camilo José Cela, *Christ versus Arizona.*
The Family of Pascual Duarte.
The Hive.
Louis-Ferdinand Céline, *Castle to Castle.*
Conversations with Professor Y.
London Bridge.
Normance.
North.
Rigadoon.
Hugo Charteris, *The Tide Is Right.*
Jerome Charyn, *The Tar Baby.*
Eric Chevillard, *Demolishing Nisard.*
Marc Cholodenko, *Mordechai Schamz.*
Joshua Cohen, *Witz.*
Emily Holmes Coleman, *The Shutter of Snow.*
Robert Coover, *A Night at the Movies.*
Stanley Crawford, *Log of the S.S. The Mrs Unguentine.*
Some Instructions to My Wife.
Robert Creeley, *Collected Prose.*
René Crevel, *Putting My Foot in It.*
Ralph Cusack, *Cadenza.*
Susan Daitch, *L.C.*
Storytown.
Nicholas Delbanco, *The Count of Concord.*
Sherbrookes.
Nigel Dennis, *Cards of Identity.*
Peter Dimock, *A Short Rhetoric for Leaving the Family.*
Ariel Dorfman, *Konfidenz.*
Coleman Dowell, *The Houses of Children.*
Island People.
Too Much Flesh and Jabez.
Arkadii Dragomoshchenko, *Dust.*
Rikki Ducornet, *The Complete Butcher's Tales.*
The Fountains of Neptune.
The Jade Cabinet.
The One Marvelous Thing.
Phosphor in Dreamland.
The Stain.
The Word "Desire."
William Eastlake, *The Bamboo Bed.*
Castle Keep.
Lyric of the Circle Heart.
Jean Echenoz, *Chopin's Move.*
Stanley Elkin, *A Bad Man.*
Boswell: A Modern Comedy.
Criers and Kibitzers, Kibitzers and Criers.
The Dick Gibson Show.
The Franchiser.
George Mills.
The Living End.
The MacGuffin.
The Magic Kingdom.
Mrs. Ted Bliss.
The Rabbi of Lud.
Van Gogh's Room at Arles.
Annie Ernaux, *Cleaned Out.*
Lauren Fairbanks, *Muzzle Thyself.*
Sister Carrie.
Leslie A. Fiedler, *Love and Death in the American Novel.*
Juan Filloy, *Op Oloop.*
Gustave Flaubert, *Bouvard and Pécuchet.*
Kass Fleisher, *Talking out of School.*
Ford Madox Ford, *The March of Literature.*
Jon Fosse, *Aliss at the Fire.*
Melancholy.
Max Frisch, *I'm Not Stiller.*
Man in the Holocene.

SELECTED DALKEY ARCHIVE PAPERBACKS

SELECTED DALKEY ARCHIVE PAPERBACKS

My Life in CIA.
Singular Pleasures.
The Sinking of the Odradek Stadium.
Tlooth.
20 Lines a Day.
JOSEPH MCELROY,
Night Soul and Other Stories.
THOMAS MCGONIGLE,
Going to Patchogue.
ROBERT L. MCLAUGHLIN, ED., *Innovations: An Anthology of Modern & Contemporary Fiction.*
ABDELWAHAB MEDDEB, *Talismano.*
HERMAN MELVILLE, *The Confidence-Man.*
AMANDA MICHALOPOULOU, *I'd Like.*
STEVEN MILLHAUSER,
The Barnum Museum.
In the Penny Arcade.
RALPH J. MILLS, JR.,
Essays on Poetry.
MOMUS, *The Book of Jokes.*
CHRISTINE MONTALBETTI, *Western.*
OLIVE MOORE, *Spleen.*
NICHOLAS MOSLEY, *Accident.*
Assassins.
Catastrophe Practice.
Children of Darkness and Light.
Experience and Religion.
God's Hazard.
The Hesperides Tree.
Hopeful Monsters.
Imago Bird.
Impossible Object.
Inventing God.
Judith.
Look at the Dark.
Natalie Natalia.
Paradoxes of Peace.
Serpent.
Time at War.
The Uses of Slime Mould: Essays of Four Decades.
WARREN MOTTE,
Fables of the Novel: French Fiction since 1990.
Fiction Now: The French Novel in the 21st Century.
Oulipo: A Primer of Potential Literature.
YVES NAVARRE, *Our Share of Time.*
Sweet Tooth.
DOROTHY NELSON, *In Night's City.*
Tar and Feathers.
ESHKOL NEVO, *Homesick.*
WILFRIDO D. NOLLEDO, *But for the Lovers.*
FLANN O'BRIEN,
At Swim-Two-Birds.
At War.
The Best of Myles.
The Dalkey Archive.
Further Cuttings.
The Hard Life.
The Poor Mouth.
The Third Policeman.
CLAUDE OLLIER, *The Mise-en-Scène.*
Wert and the Life Without End.
PATRIK OUŘEDNÍK, *Europeana.*
The Opportune Moment, 1855.
BORIS PAHOR, *Necropolis.*
FERNANDO DEL PASO,
News from the Empire.
Palinuro of Mexico.
ROBERT PINGET, *The Inquisitory.*
Mahu or The Material.
Trio.
MANUEL PUIG,
Betrayed by Rita Hayworth.
The Buenos Aires Affair.
Heartbreak Tango.
RAYMOND QUENEAU, *The Last Days.*
Odile.
Pierrot Mon Ami.
Saint Glinglin.
ANN QUIN, *Berg.*
Passages.
Three.
Tripticks.
ISHMAEL REED,
The Free-Lance Pallbearers.
The Last Days of Louisiana Red.
Ishmael Reed: The Plays.
Juice!
Reckless Eyeballing.
The Terrible Threes.
The Terrible Twos.
Yellow Back Radio Broke-Down.
JOÃO UBALDO RIBEIRO, *House of the Fortunate Buddhas.*
JEAN RICARDOU, *Place Names.*
RAINER MARIA RILKE, *The Notebooks of Malte Laurids Brigge.*
JULIÁN RÍOS, *The House of Ulysses.*
Larva: A Midsummer Night's Babel.
Poundemonium.
Procession of Shadows.
AUGUSTO ROA BASTOS, *I the Supreme.*
DANIËL ROBBERECHTS,
Arriving in Avignon.
JEAN ROLIN, *The Explosion of the Radiator Hose.*
OLIVIER ROLIN, *Hotel Crystal.*
ALIX CLEO ROUBAUD, *Alix's Journal.*
JACQUES ROUBAUD, *The Form of a City Changes Faster, Alas, Than the Human Heart.*
The Great Fire of London.
Hortense in Exile.
Hortense Is Abducted.
The Loop.
The Plurality of Worlds of Lewis.
The Princess Hoppy.
Some Thing Black.
LEON S. ROUDIEZ, *French Fiction Revisited.*
RAYMOND ROUSSEL, *Impressions of Africa.*
VEDRANA RUDAN, *Night.*
STIG SÆTERBAKKEN, *Siamese.*
LYDIE SALVAYRE, *The Company of Ghosts.*
Everyday Life.
The Lecture.
Portrait of the Writer as a Domesticated Animal.
The Power of Flies.
LUIS RAFAEL SÁNCHEZ,
Macho Camacho's Beat.
SEVERO SARDUY, *Cobra & Maitreya.*
NATHALIE SARRAUTE,
Do You Hear Them?
Martereau.
The Planetarium.